INTO SHADOW FOREST

A FANTASY NOVEL

SWORD MASTER OF HONEY HEART RESORT

JONATHAN EVAN HUDSON

INTO SHADOW FOREST

CHAPTER 1
ROMEO

Romeo Bladell knew there shouldn't be a rope bridge crossing the canyon here yet …

Here it was.

And the canyon itself was a deep jagged gash in the granite. Actually, more like how the maw of a deep gray dragon was.

(Not that he'd ever seen a dragon of any sort, but maybe one day …)

The canyon itself was only a few good times wider than he was tall—but he wasn't exactly tall, and now that he was in his late twenties, it was long past the time where he'd get any taller.

The posts the ropes were tied to were stout logs. They only went up to his knees, but they still reminded him of his stout dwarven grandpa, whose bald head, even when he was on his toes, could only reach the tips of Romeo's chest.

But ... the logs looked older than some of the thick craggy oaks behind him. You know, the kind of oaks so old the moss of them doubled as old guy beards.

No, dwarf beards.

The planks were light gray and as warped as the weird joke the world had to be playing on him. The occasional gust of wind was refreshingly cool, like a lemonade during a hot summer day—like today actually, it was hotter than a hot spring with a roasting rock tossed in, so the gusts were more than welcome.

Each gust also made all four ropes of the bridge crackle out as loud as the crows in the bearded oaks behind him.

The bridge was even sunken a bit by the middle.

Like a sly bridgy smile—at the joke being played on him.

He was a lean and mean five foot six, so yes, he was a bit on the short side, for a human, but compared to dwarves, he was on the taller side, and he was muscular enough to wear his red jerkin like a vest, with no shirt, and his brown slacks were snug, but not tight.

Rather than risk another pair of flimsy sandals breaking again, he went with his reliable suede boots. They were dark red and the darkness was not entirely from the dirt of use. They were like thick reliable socks. Thick enough to protect his feet yet he could still easily feel the soggy soil underneath them.

Feel the few smooth pebbles in the soil.

Maybe climb down the canyon but ... the sides of the canyon were steep cliffs. At the bottom it would be incredibly slippery. It would take another hour or two. No. More like three. Assuming the light lasted. Longer if it didn't.

Much longer—and for what?

His backpack was basically a big bag with shoulder straps. It was made from sturdy burlap but far from water proof. It had some long-awaited precious books—more than a few of those books were the latest dime dreadfuls meant for guests, but he got to read them first to ensure there weren't any obvious problems. There were more than a few bottles of absolutely needed olive oil for lamps and cooking. Most important of all, some general provisions for the next few days.

Get the provision wet ... and not just the books ... yikes.

But Romeo ... the hackles on his neck stood up just looking at the odd bridge. It seemed to promise the hope of saving him over two hours. The usual bridge was an arch of stone along the paved usual road, but it crossed the river below long after the canyon was no longer a canyon.

And that bridge was well over another few hours hike away.

This shortcut, hiking along the canyon already saved him a few hours since the regular road made a very wide curve around the forest behind him.

All because rumors of monsters in there, but they were just rumors. Yup. Still, the bearded oaks behind were a part of the fringe of what was known as Shadow Forest and he had seen some of the corpses of the beasts in there ... like horse-sized blue jays called jumping raptors and ...

No.

They and the other dangerous beasts were only found much further south, much deeper in the forest, not here, in the fringes, at the edge of the civilized world.

In fact, that hint of danger was a draw to the Honey Heart Resort. Honey Heart Resort was a spring bath inn and resort on top of the mountain here where Romeo was working at for the past few years.

Sigh.

So as Uncle Jethron would say, trust your nose when all else fails, and Uncle Jethron was among the best trackers in the county—human and dwarf.

So ...

CHAPTER 2
ROMEO

... *S*niff. Sniff.

The smell ... earthy soil. Mossy oak like all forests everywhere. The cool crisp clean smell of the river below. Echoes of the splashes and crashing of foamy rapids splashing against unyielding rock. Echoes snapping against the canyon's steep sides.

The usual smells. Sounds.

The midday rain had washed away his own footsteps from the morning trip. The crazy heat had already dried out the soil enough for it not to be outright muddy.

Just damp.

In fact, the wooden posts showed the usual expected grim from the ages.

You'd think the bridge had been here for ages too.

But it hadn't.

This very morning, on the way to town, back when the taste of his latest experimental pine needle tea was burning his mouth far too bitter, there hadn't been any rope bridge here at all.

Along the cliff on the other side of the canyon, the lichen showed no scraps along the jagged rock cliffs—no sign of any climber involved in setting up the bridge.

And Romeo read enough books over the years to know what's involved.

Rope would of been secured on one side of the canyon, and the climber climb down, go cross the foamy rapids by jumping the slimy slippery rocks, and climb up and stake the ropes on the other side.

In fact, Romeo had done such work as a side job here and there.

Another, more straightforward approach was to shoot arrows with rope tied to the ends into one of the trees beyond the canyon. Someone else on the other side would then tie the rope to the post.

Or if a heavier rope was needed, only a lighter rope would be shot and secured to the trees on both sides of the canyon. The thicker rope would be carried over and tied to posts on each side.

But ... no matter how much Romeo studied the line of bearded craggy oaks on the other side, there wasn't a sign of torn moss, of any arrows shot into their bark, or even a sign that the dirt was disturbed in the slightest.

Looking up at the sky, mostly blue with some clouds, but ... less than a few hours to sunset.

Legends said monsters were most active after night, and this close to Shadow Forest ...

Getting to the road ... he might not make it back in time.

Aunt Tilda would. be. *pissed.*

She was as big as ma, being her older sister and all, and she was the kind of women a guy would sprint a few laps around, as a woman should be, would be what pa would say, and grandpa, but ... ugh.

He really to get back before sundown.

Aunt Tilda was the boss lady of Honey Heart Resort, and he knew there were more than enough provisions for the night. For the next morning ... enough. Aunt Tilda could scrap enough together to last a couple more days but ... sigh.

Lucky for him it was Tuesday, not Monday. Tuesday was the slowest time of the week, even now, during the peak of summer, the hottest and busiest season.

But Romeo also knew this path wasn't commonly taken. Few even knew of it. Most travelers would take the long winding road rather than risk whatever trouble the fringes of Shadow Forest may throw at them. Rumors of monsters and worse things ...

Sigh. Would Aunt Tilda believe him about this bridge?

Even if she did, she'd absolutely forbid him from taking any "short-cut" (or "long-cut" as she'd call it then) off the road ever again.

(One sister and his foolish hubby lost was enough, she'd say, she wasn't about to risk her dear nephew, the last of her flesh and blood ...)

And ... honestly, it's unlikely anyone else would even run

into this rope bridge. No other witnesses. This place was so ... empty ... so ... weird ... weird place for a trap but deep down ...

CHAPTER 3
ROMEO

Sigh.

Romeo had to scratch his hair. It needed a good scratching, and his hand was a good a comb as any. It was short and black and untamed as he wanted to be but … sigh.

No worries if he got it a little soiled.

Like those stakes.

They even had splatters of soil right by the ground. The rain was around midday so the earliest this bridge could of appeared was sometime late in the morning.

The sweet aftertaste of that last lemonade at town at the cafe known as Honey's End … lemon juice with loads of honey, utterly brilliant … and his tab was due next time he stopped by. A penny for each … and way too many lemonades this summer, but they also carried the latest and greatest dime dreadfuls.

Should he take off his bag and take a break? Think things over? It was a bit heavy and his shoulders ...

Of course it was. As it should be.

With a few days of provisions for the personal at the Honey Heart Resort, besides the bunch of bottles of olive oil for the lamps and more than a few books. His shoulders ached, but he didn't regret avoiding a shirt today. The heat was bad enough with the vest on. He'd go with shorts but if, for some reason, he needed to dash through the woods ... no.

Slacks it was.

The bearded oaks behind him didn't hide any dangers, usually, but just in case, strapped to his belt was the harpe blade he inherited from pa. It was curved like a crescent moon. The metal was still clean and reflective as a mirror. Only the inner edge was sharp, but that edge was rumored to be sharp enough to slice through steel.

But how ... Romeo hadn't figure it out yet.

He couldn't even cut through the black granite of this mountain range yet. Practice practice practice yet ...

Especially against the occasional cocky patron, as Aunt Tilda permitted, no, insisted, putting his swords skills to good safe work, and, of course, as she insisted, he let those patrons win just enough keep their ego more than intact.

Or more often, have Romeo spar against the bubble cute and gorgeous Vivian, with her long lush rosy pink hair and forever rosy smell, yet wow, did she have a way with her double sabers.

Ouch.

Graceful hourglass to a boy's doom, was one way to put

it, and true be told, when they sparred, she didn't exactly hate him.

No.

If he didn't know better, and one couldn't hide their true feelings behind a clash of blades, as his pa would say, Vivian, maybe, had some feelings for Romeo.

The good kind.

Feelings Aunt Tilda clearly didn't approve of, or else she would of allowed Romeo to spend more time than just the random but dramatic sparring match against Vivian.

Match more or less meant to convince patrons Vivian, despite her gorgeous looks and vividly dramatic moves, she was definitely a stunning great swordsgal. So when she let those cocky patrons defeat her, wow, they must be like totally, *awe***some**, as Vivian would always say, and always so cutesy happy too.

And her bright violet eyes were always smiling around him too. Unlike many of the patrons that ogled her extra hefty bosom as she jiggled it plenty.

Especially to distract Romeo during a bout.

But ... rumor had it his own very blade, his harpe, had cut down legendary monsters like hobgobbles, clawgirls and even dragotrolls back back and back centuries ago back when the legendary enemies of mankind, the monsters known as the baelzog, those winged titans of fire and shadow, nearly flooded the whole entire world with guess what, shadow and flame (and monsters, many many monsters the human-munching sort, which lead to the question, once humanity was gone, what would all those monsters munch?)

Like any decent adventure-loving guy, he had seen his fill of illustrations of each and every one those monsters.

Who hadn't?

Every dime dreadful worth its dime had more than a few and Romeo read his fair share of them and what kind of guy would he be if he didn't know anything about them?

With Shadow Forest so near, this place should of been ripe for adventure. The Honey Heart Resort drew more than a few patrons because of it and that's one reason Aunt Tilda built the resort here, of all places, as she admitted more than once, (but before she lost her sister and ...)

While the honey hearts who lived and worked at honey heart resort were the stunningly gorgeous girls whose company the patrons came to enjoy along with the hot springs ...

Those honey hearts were pure damsels-in-distress-to-be, at least in the minds of lusty patrons, and Aunt Tilda paid good coin to the girls' families, and to the girls to work there for a living, at least until their youthful looks faded — or a patron paid amazing coin to marry one, but few bothered to actually marry ...

When Romeo first came to this vast mountain range of the blackest of granite, he could easily imagine secret hordes of hobgobbles lurking in some of those vast caves or among those craggy peaks.

And hobgobbles, the sword fodder of the monster minion lot, they have slimy blue skin, a big round head with only a massive fanged maw, yet their sight was somehow amazingly good, and even more messed up, they had powerful tentacles for arms and legs. They supposedly stunk like dead fish and sniiiiiff.

Mossy oak. Earthy soil. River rapids.

Nope. No hobgobbles nearby.

Like always.

Phew.

If there were any hobgobbles around, they must love staying in their rumored nests deep deep deeeeeeep inside those caves that Romeo never had the chance to explore.

Yet.

Rumors of hobgobbles here and there throughout the realm, well, some bounties were actually paid for confirmed kills, according to the patrons here and there, and since some of those patrons doing the talking were also doing the paying … (as in paying the bounties …)

Now clawgirls got caught more often.

They were gorgeous human girls in one form, so they took far more risks to actual mingle with humans, but their other form was their true evil reptilian self.

Instead of skin, they could shift their skin into protective but gorgeous scales which, even now, would fetch more than a few pretty pennies.

Instead of hands and feet, they had beastly but beautiful lizard talons with gorgeous but wicked deadly claws.

And that's why they were called clawgirls.

They played the honey pot role in stories everywhere and they were also (sometimes) wicked cruel archers too, supposedly, in their human form, but all in all, they were often fodder sent to raze through armed men because no armor could deflect their razor claws, and thus, another reason why they were called clawgirls, not talongirls.

Some stories even claimed their claws were poisoned.

Or had other wicked powers in their claws.

Patrons confirmed it all here and there. Bounties they themselves paid in silver. Not copper pennies. Like the copper Aunt Tilda paid him every other week. *Silvers.*

Real serious money.

And plenty more clawgirls were still hiding. Even after all these centuries. Waiting for their chance to strike.

Avenge their lost sisters.

(And a dime dreadful wasn't a dime dreadful without some wickedly gorgeous clawgirl going femme fatale with her amazingly unique and deadly claw power.)

But ... a clawgirl out in the middle of nowhere ... ha!

Keep dreaming.

(Not even the patrons dreamed that far.)

Anyway, clawgirls were still girls and cutting one down ... even if she was a wicked monster ... ugh.

Better face a dragotrolls, and the dragotrolls were the real captains of terror. They were like a cross between a massive deformed man and dragon. Even better, they were as several times fiercer than the dragons they rode as mounts.

He'd know if there was a dragotroll nearby and there wasn't.

Good.

No bounties collected on them in his lifetime, but the occasional "disaster" as patrons would call them ... well, disaster within their lifetime ...

Unlike any baelzog.

No hint of them, and they were titans. Giants. Winged giants and all shadow, smoke, and flame.

The forest would be on fire if any of them were around.

None had been spotted outside of dime dreadfuls for centuries.

Over a thousand years or so.

It was best that way too.

And sure, the handy work at the resort kept his body in shape for when destiny called, if ever, and sure, he often turned chores into secretive training and ended up completing the tasks far soon and far better than any other handy man could hope to.

But maybe … Romeo could take a break … to train, some.

(You never know what a monster from legend would pop up and cause havoc.)

((Even a clawgirl.))

(((Or a honey heart turned out to be an evil clawgirl in disguise then … nah. Keep dreaming. She'd just then be considered exotic goods.)))

((((Maybe.))))

CHAPTER 4
JULIET

Juliet swore she smelled a familiar hint of spoiled fish.

Her skin right new felt its freshest and cleanest in ages and just that hint made her want to cringe but no, she strutted in her stilettos high and proud like a claw-girl hiding perfectly in sight.

As long as that smell wasn't what she knew it was.

The ground was soft but not muddy. It scrapped as loud as the river down below in the canyon, and the only reason she even went this way. So far out of the way. She needed to shed her skin again and where better to dump her serpent skin than here?

In the middle of nowhere forest.

The trees were so big ... Boss Tilda even had the beds of the honey hearts as the stumps of those big trees, and wow, were those beds huuuge. The lichen was here was still green and crumbly rather than green and silky from the pricy, magical treatments Boss Tilda put on their beds.

Since, eventually, now that she was eighteen … she'd be using it to … for patrons … enjoyment … as well.

(Gulp.)

Sure, right now she looked like the part of a gorgeous honey heart. Six sexy feet of peaches and cream complexion and strawberries and cream scent, both as sweet on the eyes and nose as on the loins—well, loins once the bidding for her virginity … gulp.

But she was eighteen today. Big girl time.

This life was faaaar better than wandering the woods as some crazed clawgirl eager to avenge her sister for things dead and gone.

And a good virginity auction should help pay off her debt far sooner, and Juliet would get a cut of it to hold onto. Keep with the rest of her coin in her heart-shaped pouch and its many protective spells.

A pouch she kept strapped to her slim waist.

Her outfit wasn't so bad in this crazy heat, actually. Being scantily clad, just like she was expected to be, had it perks during the summer, after all!

Her top was a bra top of a pair of blue hearts cupped her breasts with stretchy soft blue silk, and best of all, they were the biggest moneymaking breasts at Honey Heart Resort. Her miniskirt was also a pair of blue hearts strapped together with the stretchiest white silk, and they were upside down for just enough coverage that patron only needed to undress her a little with their eyes.

How her miniskirt fit so snug yet so comfortable over her crotch and behind, leaving only the sides of her hips bare ... yet never showing anything underneath ... a magical pentacle woven on the underside of the hearts.

Thank Boss Tilda to insist on no fashion mishaps.

No free peeks.

Juliet hadn't shifted in ages. Her reptilian form felt so ... different, yet it really wasn't. Her skin went to exotically pink scales. Her neon blue eyes went serpent and sigh.

Even if the pink scales she shed washed up somewhere, the skin of pink scales might still be worth so much some hunters would come searching for the clawgirl who shed them but ... Juliet wasn't stupid.

That Prince was wrong *wrong* **wrong!**

She let him win on purpose, of course, like she always did, but now, if only a rematch, if only he'd come back, she could prove she wasn't some dumb blonde who spent too time on her ass-long golden hair which ... her hair was really scales so she couldn't really trim it easily without ... magic to shrink it.

Cutting them ... ouchie ouchie ouchie — never again!

Ah!

That fish stink ... hobgobbles.

As a clawgirl, she'd need to command them to ... no. Avoid them.

Avoid them at all costs.

That dragotroll might of sent them to find her. Summon her.

After all, her claws' power might be one of the keys needed to unlocking their ancient masters, the Baelzog.

As if she wanted more masters.

Boss Tilda was bad enough but least ... life here wasn't so bad. It was nice, really, and that boy Romeo ... she even, sort of, made a friend, sort of.

He was as short as a hobgobble, and not too bright, but unlike the other girls, he always played games with her without insulting her or unlike those lustsmitten patrons, drown her with fake compliments.

If only the patrons could be more like him but no ... that Prince ... if only he'd ... no, keep dreaming.

A flash of blue across the canyon?

Oh no.

Juliet hissed. "Leave me be!"

She could *feel* her eyes go serpent. It pinched so, so cozy yet so ...

Stupid stupid stupid!

Never go serpent eyed!

That's a dead clawgirl give away, and she really might end up dead!

Chuckles rang out from across the canyon. A hobgobble a good bit taller and brawnier than Romeo slipped out. Flashes of big suggested even more were staying hidden.

"Mustress," the hobgobble said, "Return with us."

His voice had that watery gurgle accent that most hobgobbles had, but somehow, she could easily understand him.

And this one was clearly a him. How she knew ... she had no idea.

But even her sisters way back when could too.

Without knowing how.

"Too dangerous," Juliet said, "I—"

"Hunting human boy?" the hobgobble said, "Gud. Need practice. Scouts say bridge up ahead. Meet there. We shall soften boy up for you."

Human boy? Oh no. How could it be? But ... showing mercy toward a human ... around them no less ...

"Firssst to catch him," Juliet said, "Gets a share cooked by yourssss truly."

Ack! She was hissing without meaning to. Damn, was she nervous about this femme fatale clawgirl stuff, but asking them to spare the boy would only get him killed quicker and crueler.

Better she hurry up ahead and warn the boy quick.

Help him get away.

There wasn't a bridge for a few hours. Maybe no need to ... who was she kidding.

She better hurry. Thank Boss Tilda she trained all honey hearts to hurry in these stupid stilettos.

Even some self-defense. Since the heel were practically daggers.

"Fressh boy meat," she said, "Nothing betterssss!"

And dashed like her own life was on the line.

(*Despite* the stilettos ...)

CHAPTER 5
ROMEO

Double sigh.

Maybe ... Romeo could go a bit into the woods ... and practice on the mossy trees. They were more than big enough to take it, and their mossy beards needed a trim.

Yes. He should. Practice that special sword technique. The new one. Puributcher he dubbed it.

Get Vivian dirty. In battle.

Then clean her off perfectly.

Including her clothes. A disrobing of the perfect kind.

His cheeks blazed at the thought, but the way Vivian teased him so much during their sparring bouts, the way she sliced and nicked him so suggestively that he had to fight in his linens more often than not ... time for some vengeance.

The kind she'd appreciate.

But he couldn't use it in battle, not yet, let alone against Vivian, until he practiced it plenty. Until using it was second nature.

Never mind the rumors of tree monsters.

Even if it was Shadow Forest, after all, the fringes of it, and everyone said even the fringes were dangerous to wander off into.

It's not like the wood would dull his blade, or even dirty its reflective surface, because unlike most blades, his harpe would never grow dull because, according to pa, and pa did teach him more than just the basics but ... after pa and ma vanished years ago ...

No. Near a decade ago by now.

Ever since Romeo went over to his Aunt Tilda he had to earn his own keep the honest hard-working way and going swordmaster meant risking getting crippled useless like Uncle One-leg Jethron who also, supposedly, used to have some sword skills of his own but ...

Okay. Wandering into Shadow Forest, even to practice bladework, a good stupid way to end up vanishing, and Aunt Tilda couldn't handle losing her nephew the very same way she lost her sister.

It was why she was forcefully against him using his bladework to earn coin.

Beyond the fixed game with a patron she carefully overseered. And that was only when Vivian was too busy with patrons otherwise. According to Aunt Tilda, he'd better keep to safe reliable handy work and live a long safe life ... but ... Romeo ... he wasn't sure if ... it was the right thing to do but ...

Caw caw caw — the crows behind him were shocked and ?!

Across the canyon — Romeo couldn't believe his own lying eyes but …

CHAPTER 6
CLAUDIA

Claudia Killjoy savored the smell of human blood in her red wine. Nothing filled a water skin quite like red wine spiced with human blood preserved right. It always had just the right iron bite.

A bite as sharp as the crimson iron blades on her arrows.

And her arrows would need all the bite they could give today. For today she wasn't just another overly lovely human girl going archer, but a clawgirl finally marching proud against the human menace.

Today her thick leather thigh boots were also sandals that had space for her slim feet to transform into proper talons, and yet remained a stylish sleek ruby just like her long lush hair that far too many filthy human men leered at.

And the bracken in this place kept slapping her legs and behind almost as badly as the human men she once fought alongside.

Men now dead from the hobgobbles who claimed her. Yes. Clawgirls like her had failed their masters so badly that hobgobbles now could command clawgirls.

It was enough to make her blood run colder than the river down in that canyon nearby.

At least it was hot enough, even in the shade of the thick winding oaks, that her wine was all but steaming hot and yet still refreshing.

But not hot enough.

Her fingerless elbow gloves, as sleek and stylishly ruby as they were, they also let her transform her slim hands into talons as well, but now, she needed permission to transform, even to change her lovely green eyes to go serpent slitted. So forget using the power of her claws to heat the wine up even more.

Forget adding flames to anything.

At least her mouth cloth and cowled hood hid her sour expression. Not that any of the hobgobbles' stink, their rotten fish stink would curl her lips any poutier than they were. It was bad enough that this leotard showed too much of her chest and stomach, as if saying feather her there.

So what if it was stylishly sleek and red?

Even if her skin in her human form was still protective scales, very very veeeery fine scales, they weren't as protective in this form. She wasn't due for another shedding soon either. So any wound would be … awfully visible.

As if the hobgobbles were … no. She was that expendable, was she?

Her sister Fleur was at least still beside her. Dunned in

the same sleek outfit of a scandalous leotard, elbow gloves, and thigh sandal boots, but all in lightning blue to match her talon's water powers. She was trying to comb the twigs and leaves from her long lush wind-blown sunny hair. Again. Her hood was off. Again. Her big blue eyes so wide and terrified.

"Will …" Fleur said, "we really need to … kill him?"

Her thirst for blood, human blood, never as great as Claudia's, even back when Fleur had a legendary lust for battle.

"Yessss," Claudia said, "even if he's a cutie pie."

Fleur tugged one of her curlier locks.

"I know …" Fleur said, "but …"

Claudia patted her sister's quiver. It was just as full as Claudia's. Same arrows. Same bows. Human bone scimitars joined by the handle, so their bows doubled as long range and short-range weapons.

"We're clawgirls," Claudia said, "Time to end the human menace. One human at a time, if need be."

Fleur gulped. "One human at a time."

Yet she cringed. Figures. Such a mousey clawgirl.

"Or Masssster Hobgobble …" Fleur said.

"We can't go back to the resort," Claudia said, "Massster inisssted we …"

Fleur nodded. "The patrons mussst die next. Quick. Not painful, but they … they were right about usss, weren't they?"

Claudia almost snarled, almost, but instead, she only yanked Fleur's hood and mouth cloth back over her heart of a face.

"Our virginity auction was going well," Claudia said, "too well, until Massster Hobgobble—"

"I know," Fleur said, "now we owe him for …"

Fleur stood up. Six feet of gorgeous blonde some men were willing to pay a fortune to be the first to deflower. Even more than Claudia herself.

Now they were all dead. As they deserved.

Their small fortunes now in the heart of a pouch strapped to the clawgirl who they would of dared to defile.

Still, only Juliet might of commanded more and that bitch Juliet …

"Don't worry," Fleur said, "we'll catch Juliet. She'll join usss jusst like … and then our true masssters … let's find that bridge before the other hobgobbles. Maybe … young boy … tasstes good?"

Claudia chuckled. Stood up beside her sister. Smiling proud.

"Now you're thinking right," Claudia said, "We can't let Juliet have all the boy killing fun, can we?"

"The village," Fleur said, "Then the world."

"Yup," Claudia said, "Once our next true master here is revived."

Fleur nodded, but those wide terrified eyes …

Only a matter of time before they were no longer terrified.

But full of bloodthirsty glee.

CHAPTER 7
ROMEO

Romeo couldn't even gasp. Since across the canyon … this gash of a canyon …

Passed the grassy ledge of dark soil …

Across the long smile of a rope bridge …

Deep passed the bearded oaks whispering their planty curses at whatever trees loved cursing at …

And where the murk was darker than his chances of a date with any heart honey ever … in the glimpses of massive boulders jutting out the ground …

A hint of blue!

A blue as dark as soiled blueberries, or like the blueberries ma once left out too long before making blueberry crumb pie and …

The blue even had the same slimy look of those rotten blueberries.

Hobgobbles?

(Finally!)

Wait, the smells ... sniff, sniff. Bearded oaks. Sniff. River rapids ... earthy soil. Sniff.

And rotting fish!

Romeo drew his harpe quick.

"You want trouble?" he said, "You found it!"

Chuckles came from across the canyon.

From three hobgobbles. They slithered out of the woods.

And wow, they were just like the dime dreadfuls illustrated them.

Big blue heads with no hint of eyes or ears yet their sight and hearing, (supposedly) amazing. All three had big maws with jagged teeth and no doubt an endless hunger for flesh of the innocent.

From their big heads each had over a dozen thick blue and powerful tentacles. All their tentacles had hooked suckers eager to tear into helpless prey. Half of the tentacles doubled as legs, and the other as arms. Each of the three carried several dark wicked spears.

Spears ridged like the mouth of a pike.

The biggest of the three, the one ahead of the other two, it must be the leader. It gurgled a growl. Like a challenge or ...

"I swear on Krakegus EldRiguth," it said, "Give us gurl and die gud death. Resist and gut eaten slooow and ulive."

It even spoke like the dime dreadfuls, but wait, girl?

"Die?" Romeo said, "Ha! You first."

It flung a spear right at his chest.

So quick.

But Romeo was quicker. Harpe out.

And CLANK!

Deflected—no!

The power of the spear deflected him.

THUNK!

From far behind him. The spear into one of the trees.

"To deflect my gulgen spear," the leader said, "That blade, not an ordinary one. I claim it."

"Too bad," Romeo said, "You want it? Come and take it!"

The leader motioned his two followers. They both flung a spear.

Almost as quick. At each of his shoulders.

And too quick to dodge completely.

But Romeo—quicker.

He whipped his harp up. Shielded his shoulders with it. Ducked down just enough that—

CLANK CLANK!

Deflected them up.

Him back back and back. CRACK.

Into a bearded oak. **Hard**.

THUNK THUNK!

His shoulder, his back, painfully bruised, but his training through his hard labor for Aunt Tilda, thankfully, they weren't broken.

Yet.

Time for a secret sword technique. The first he ever learned. Mastered.

And make his pa proud.

CHAPTER 8
ROMEO

Bearded oak to his back, Romeo focused on the eerie silence.

Not a single crow caw anywhere.

Not rustle from a stray cool breeze. Not in this hot spring heat without the spring.

No.

The silence his pa trained him to embrace. Treat his own heart thunks as the steady powerful music of battle.

And with this heat bathing him with sweat ...

Thump thump thump.

His grip on his harpe was still more than solid enough.

A deep breath. Rotting fish galore.

Thump thump thump.

But the ground, it was still muddy slick. Any solid blow could made him slip. Good thing his suede boots let his toes grip the ground as solidly as they could. Some stray pebbles helped, so luck was on his side.

Thump thump thump.

Like a dance to doom, thump thump, flow—thump—with it, thump, flow—thump—into it, thump thump, become it.

Thump thump **thump SLASH!**

A slash that glowed bluer than the sky.

Ripped through the air like a lightning bolt.

Smashed into the hobgobbles spears and exploded.

BOOOOOM!!!

Blowing them away them. Even their spears.

Pa would be proud of his Slash-o-Boom Technique.

CHAPTER 9

JAGGER

With his broadsword dug deep and secure in the rocky soil, Jagger Vondin stood his full six strong feet right at the edge of this steep canyon. Stared deep into its dark churning depths.

The smell of fresh river rapids came from below. A hint of fish here and there. Of the green slime on the boulders jutting out of the rapids, and on the rock hemming the rapids in.

Of course, the musty earthy but familiar smell of moist forest. Shadow Forest here, not so different from other forest, except for a few trails of beasts he didn't recognize. One similar to blue jays, but with far more predatory rotting flesh smell to it. Another of deer, but with a burning sensation similar to the burn of the coldest ice.

Even one of rotting fish.

Of squid.

No doubt hobgobbles. Many of them.

A party of them, over a dozen of them, passed this very spot by quite recently. Right beyond the trail. Along the top of this canyon. Within the mossy trees.

With them, the smell of thick leather made from human skin, and water warped wood, and steel, which meant the usual harpoons and spears.

And they weren't the only ones.

Disturbing, but not unheard of for such a barren region.

The smell of crows cawing for rotting flesh. Crows were smart enough to know when they'd soon be well fed, and that smell of excitement ...

They knew a feast was coming.

The smell of fearful squirrels and songbirds. Common smells in any forest, but the musk of a young human man in leather, suede, and cotton, and a zing like a spray up the nose, a magical blade of some sort.

Then a girl ... strongly of strawberries and cream, a solid hint of cherries and vanilla, and of silk and cotton, but that faint smell of chemical almonds and feline — hark!

Her outfit was woven from that famous fabric known as nyalon, a coveted fabric from the distant East because it could stretched so well, yet stay so snug against the body, yet breathed so well that the girl didn't sweat in the slightest.

The zing of magic in the fabric ... no wonder the girl wasn't sweating.

There was also leather with her, but far more processed than the man's, and that zing of magic, quite a few spells woven into the leather.

He couldn't help but enjoy the scent of that young girl. No. Woman. Young woman.

But now was not the time for pleasure.

A deep breath.

A deep as his own noble bloodline.

Jagger twirled his goatee. Brushed away his long-curled hair. His hair was clean, dark and lush and smelled of it.

Good.

Even on a lone tracking, a ranger knight must look his best. Smell his best.

Common rangers would, of course, think it was mere vanity, but common ranger did not have the bloodline gift of the Bloodhound Nose.

Their presence would of only interfered.

Any other human would of.

The man and woman who passed by here, they were mere distractions, and no, they weren't together, not traveling together, maybe not even aware of each other, but close.

Another deep breath.

Jagger peered down in those dark depths. At those churning rapids. So dark. It seemed like it was only the usual river rapid. Usual boulders. Usual rock cliffs but ...

His eyes, better than any common man's, but sight could be deceptive in ways few with mere common sense could understand.

Only smells could be truly trusted.

And another smell ... so weak ... like words on the tip of his tongue ... a few feet closer.

That's all he needed.

But the tips of his thick leather boots touched the very edge of the canyon's cliff. They wouldn't dare slip on this rough ground, but their rough soles should let him find, grab a hold if worse came to worse.

His thick red slacks would protect his legs from being scrapped too bloody in the process. Adding a strong smell that may make finding the target's smell even harder.

His gloves and jerkin were a cotton and wool blend, since, as long as he cared for it properly, it wouldn't carry too strong of a smell, and they stayed the right shade of crimson, since on his chest, on the back of his gloves, the black bloodhound emblem of his House.

Of the Black Hound Clan.

And the Black Hound Clan had better quarry to hunt than a few dozen hobgobbles.

Find this prey and deal with it, and humanity may be spared the coming disaster.

So Jagger choose to risk crouching.

Crouch as low as he could go, while holding on tight to his broadsword Chaserist. Chaserist was not just solid steel, but spelled by the best alchemists to withstand both natural and unnatural elements.

To cut through them when needed.

And Chaserist's smell, from its quality magics, a full solid zing as savory as the richest steak.

No.

This was not close enough. The smells from the cliff ... he had to be sure.

Jagger leaned forward.

Over the canyon.

Using Chaserist to secure himself. Trusting his blade with his life. Not an unusual occurrence.

Lowered even more.

And more.

And ... more ...

Deeeep. Breeeath.

Sniiiiifffff.

Yes.

There it was.

Good. His quarry was near.

CHAPTER 10
ROMEO

But the smells ...

Romeo sniffed, smelled the musty bearded oaks and river rapids. Earthy soil.

No rotting anything. Not a bit of fish stink anymore.

Good.

But the wind wasn't exactly in the right direction. It was along the canyon now. If he continued on his way, the wind would again blow in his face. After a while it would get chillier than the moment after secret night dip in a cold spring.

Than that dreadful moment you got out and *ouch*, was it cold.

Caws erupted behind him ... phew.

They would be silent if there were any more hobgobbles, let alone if any were on this side of the canyon.

If anything dangerous were lurking in the bearded oaks behind him.

But the other side of the canyon ...

In the canopy, among those craggy leafy branches ... plump silent crows. Not a caw along them still.

Or even shuffle.

Just patiently waiting. For something.

It was spooky but ... he was at the fringes of Shadow Forest. He'd seen crows act weird plenty of times before and nothing came of it ...

But ... could there be more hobgobbles out there?

This wasn't a dime dreadful, but ... if the rope bridge was some sort of trap ... the hobgobbles hadn't even tried crossing it, but he couldn't think of any kind of trap it could be.

Anyway, monsters like hobgobbles would leave a trail in the lichen on the cliff, if they tried climbing down.

No sign of them on this side either.

Except for ... no, no sign of those spears.

The sky was a clear blue. Not a cloud in the sky. And this was late in the late afternoon. Sudden summer rains weren't unusual.

Even sudden thunderstorms.

And that rumble in the distance ... beyond the canopy of the bearded oaks across the canyon, ah, squint squint, the sky was a dark gray.

Thunderstorms a-coming.

He knew better than to hid under these oaks if there was lightning, but the road he was headed for had more than enough trees along its sides too. Not much cover and no decent shelter until the resort.

Forget climbing down the canyon and crossing the river. Any moment it could flash flood like the mountain streams at home and even shin-high water running fast enough was dangerous.

(He'd seen it wash away cattle and horses. As in bulls and stallions. Not just wimpy babies.)

Not that he'd dare risk crossing this strange rope bridge ...

"What are you staring at?" Juliet said, "Sheesh. Wasting time. *Again*. Don't you ever learn?"

Ah, Juliet.

That scent ... strawberries and cream with a solid hint of cherries and vanilla ... her favorite.

It didn't help that she was the most gorgeous of stunningly gorgeous honey hearts among the beauties at Honey Heart Resort. If her beauty was heat, she'd inflict fourth degree burns and on a hot day like this ... his heart racing dumb just being in her presence ... ugh.

(Could she be the girl the hobgobbles were after?)

((Hopefully ... nonono, I mean, let's hope not.)

But Romeo refused to gulp, but ... he turned ... to face her.

"Tutorial me," Romeo said, "And ... um."

To call her an A+++ university student whose only F in life was her F-cup chest was all too close to ...

"Um what?" Juliet said, "*Ass*-hole."

Let's say she stood every peachy inch of her six feet pouty and proud. She looked haughty down at him.

At every inch of the full six inches she had over his lean and short...er five foot six.

But so what? His eyes ... they were level with ...

Her top ... yes, her top.

And it was a strapless bra top. A bra made of a pair of huge heart-shaped cups. Each heart cup was blue as her big bright and intensely blue eyes.

Like blue bolts of lightning eyes.

It was the kind of top left that little to the lustiest patron's wildest imagination.

But that little, just enough.

"You ... really Juliet?" Romeo said, "Way out here ..."

He could already feel her eyes glaring bolts at him for glancing there, but so what? Her buxom bosom was practically eye level for him.

(Might as well enjoy his luck while he had it.)

(When patrons were his height, wow, did she love it, but for him ... might as get the eye-groping in when he had the excuse for it.)

Her haughty huff ... she even cocked her hips to the side and punched the sides of her hips with angry fists.

"What?" she said, "Who else would I be? *Idiot.*"

Like a sexy tight loincloth, her miniskirt was a pair of blue hearts, one upside-down heart hugging her crotch and the other her fine ass, while a couple seductively thin vanilla straps over the sides of her nearly bare thighs linked the two hearts together and kept them in strategically in place.

Even better, both hearts hung from a very **low** hanging

belt of vanilla white for that hint hint of fine virgin goods so close and so underneath.

And yet so far away.

Buttoned tight with a large pink heart.

Romeo tried a grimace. "Handy asshole to you."

Finally.

Okay, her blue stilettos looked ready to dagger his groin.

He looked up at her face and — yikes.

She scowled like her peepers could release blue bolts of lightning at his stupid ass, and not just for daring to block the obvious way across.

"You have the silvers?" she said, "I don't come cheap."

It didn't take a genius to know that her heart-shaped pouch, as in the one strapped lopsided over her slim waist held all her coin from her years here, and wow, were there protective spells on it ...

It wasn't just his hackles that shot sky high and tinkled like hell unleashed whenever he looked too long at it.

The pouch was pale blue but it was covered in so many snow-white pentacles, wow, it couldn't of been cheap to do, and Juliet was a real cheapskate. He was (partly) surprised she didn't date him simply for the freebies Aunt Tilda would toss her.

(But not *that* surprised.)

"I ..." he said and knew defeat.

He knew she never actually slept with the patrons. Not yet. She was too young.

Until today.

Today she was eighteen, so tomorrow the auction for her virginity would start and a good virginity price would reduce the time she had to pay off her debt. Aunt Tilda paid very good coin to their families for them, and the girls were expected to work it off with plenty of interest.

But the auction, it should bag more than enough coin for her to spend some time as a student the university, but not too much time, and not after she paid her debt away.

And she couldn't go until she did.

Before eighteen, Aunt Tilda allowed any of the honey hearts to avoid sex with the patrons. They also got a full day off on their birthday.

So far, Romeo knew Juliet played flirty girlfriend with a number of her "talents", which basically came down to playing with patrons like she was some ditzy, lusty girlfriend-to-be.

Like all the honey hearts, she often let them win the games just enough boost their petty egos, and they never truly realizing how much she was holding back.

(Except for a certain Prince years ago who realized it and called her too dumb for words and just another pretty face … and her fury at losing her chance to snag prince for a hubby … ugh. She was a master at some of those games now, but …)

(Worse, Romeo didn't want to admit it out loud, but those eyes of hers always were … off somehow. Sure, they seemed to look normal, no, gorgeous, yet something about them sent a cold terrifying zip up his spine.)

(Pure terror. Not lust.)

(Really.)

"Back ... some ..." he said.

Okay, he stuttered. nonsense. Same thing at this point.

Her permanent pout matched her baby face perfectly ...

Those bright red and juicy lips so matched the hint of cherries and vanilla in her strawberries and cream scent. She even cocked her hips more and punched her fists against them again.

Then leaned over.

Her scent ... so sweet and strong ... yet not eye-wateringly annoying but pleasant.

Somehow.

"Figures," Juliet said, "Us heart honeys only cater to the wealthy, remember? Not stuttering *poor* idiots. Just because we're co-workers ... don't get any funny ideas!"

Well ... at least she's honest.

The other gorgeous blondie Fleur was always sweeter than fresh strawberry pie, no matter the situation and yet never hinted whether she would ... had any ... well ... she seemed to innocent, sweet, and it wasn't just an act like it was with that redhead Claudia.

Their virginity auctions already started yesterday too, but sigh, they'd conclude at the end of this week.

So no hope of claiming Fleur for a sweetheart wify.

(And strange how Juliet's lips reminded of him the plumpest sweetest reddest strawberries he'd often get to snag for dessert when the guests often failed to finish them off.)

With another huff, Juliet batted her braided bangs that

framed her face. Her hair was as sleek and golden as the sun itself, and she let her hair grow straight down to the nap of her (mostly bare) back.

Do. not. gulp.

He gulped.

He was such an idiot. For all his sword skills, a single gorgeous girl and … Fleur was at least as awkward as Romeo whenever they were together.

As much as Claudia hated that.

As much as Fleur pretended not to know him if anyone else was presence.

Sigh. Unlike Juliet. Who didn't care who knew she knew him.

If not for her tapping her stiletto sandals louder and louder and so loud, even the crows started quieting down before she decided to use them as stiletto daggers on them instead of him.

(Ha! As if!)

(She'd never risk letting him get a free peek at her panties.)

"Geez," she said, "I don't have time for your eye-groping leering … paint a portrait and, no, on second thought, don't. Just *move*."

His throat complied by choking him silent and dumb.

She shoved him aside. That she honored him with her touch. Not even Fleur would do that.

"Idiot," she said and strutted over to the rope bridge.

He … thump thump thump, his heart thumping louder and louder, thumping at him to do something.

But what?

Her stilettos were mere steps away from stilettoing the bridge just when Romeo finally noticed what was wrong with the bridge.

Dead wrong.

CHAPTER II
CLAUDIA

The sight of a footprint jolted Claudia. It was fainter than the voice of her dear Fleur whimpering but no doubt, in the mud no less, that it had to be from a sandal.

No. A guy's suede boots.

Not a sandal.

Only Romeo wore suede boots. As much as Boss Tilda insisted he go with sandals. Since they'd wear down less frequently and cost far less.

But wasn't Romeo on the other side of the canyon?

There was some bridge here somewhere but ... oh no.

Rumbles in the distance. A thunderstorm. That would wash away any scent and trail, and make locating their first boy prey all that much harder.

Maybe impossible.

But Claudia still remembered her days as a free clawgirl. Roaming forests as dangerous as Shadow Forest here. Even in her current human form, scenting the boy, confirming it, Master Hobgobble would expect no less.

She crouched down to the ground. Careful not to let her hair and even her face, let alone her garb, touch a speck of that filthy mud.

Mouth cloth off, she took a deeeeep wide open breath. Let her tongue savor the scents.

Aaaaah.

Such a wonderful musky taste. So familiar too. that boy she loved to ignore. Loathed to acknowledge unless she had to.

Unlike her poor fool of a sister. Who clearly liked the boy. Her scent said everything. But she refused to do anything about it. Thank the Blessed Baelzog.

Boss Tilda was never ... keen on her girls dating the boy. Vivian learned that quick. Juliet ... she clearly despised the boy and that was probably the only reason Boss Tilda tolerated her ... time with him.

Unlike Fleur. Only brief here and there's.

All as awkward as a soberly virgin patron seeing a girlie nude for the first time.

At least Fleur knew her clawgirl side was ... made it too risky to embrace romance of any sort with a human. As foolish as romancing a human was in the first place. That Fleur—

"Romeo ..." Fleur said, "is closssse. I can hear Juliet."

And this time, those big blue eyes … not so terrified.

Good. Enough of Fleur's innocence. Maybe if Claudia could get Fleur to finish Romeo properly. Maybe she could realize how great killing was again. Back when they were little wormlings, Fleur was so … she loved the hunt, yet now, after so long, it's like she forgot it. Completely.

"I like, *finally* found you two."

"Vivian?" Fleur and Claudia said together.

Stepping so amazingly gracefully out from the bracken beside them, Vivian giggled, stroking her long lush hair all the way down to her slim waist, and wow, did she have the most beautifully lush and long rosy pink hair a girl could imagine. It wasn't even dyed that way either, as surprising as that sounded.

It was her natural clawgirl hair. That she managed to get away with it. Without dying it a more natural human color … sigh.

So careless. Risky but … her cutesy bubbly attitude fooled even Boss Tilda. Never mind her bright violet eyes were … rare among humans.

Claudia managed to gasp. Finally.

"What about that patron … what's his face," Claudia said, "He bought your virginity last weekend and …"

Vivi giggled sooo happy cute.

Too cute to accuse of going clawgirl, right?

"Guess, silly," Vivian said.

Uh huh.

Vivian even smelled like rosy pink roses, and her gleeful

face was that soft yet oval look with soft cheeks and lush rosy red lips that smiled sultry at them both.

More importantly, she was in the same getup as Fleur and Claudia. Except hers was also as rosy pink and beautiful as her hair.

Including her scimitar bow and quiver.

Her leotard even had a few hearts here and there. Even over those big breasts that she loved getting patrons to leer at, and unlike Juliet, she didn't hesitate to encourage it openingly by jiggling them plenty.

Fleur gasped this time.

"Massster sssaved you?" Fleur said.

"I guess save is one way to put it," Vivian said, "My patron was already a corpse puppet by the time I arrived and ... no sex for me. I get to die a clawgirl virgin. Yay!"

That jolted Fleur and Claudia both again.

"Huh?" they said together.

Claudia snorted. "I'm not going to die. Not until I kill and feast on boy flesh so much that, well ... okay, die from too much boy flesh."

Fleur stammered. "I ... d-d-don't want to die."

"Me neither," Vivian said, "but Master Hobgobble, I'm so like totally sure, has other plans. To teach us how fodder girl we are now, so better plan ahead. Right, girls?"

Vivian even strutted right up to them. No hesitation.

(Phew, but was she ... right?)

"Romeo must die," Vivian said, "Pity, he is so cute, and sweet, but silly me ..."

Claudia growled. "Don't get sentimental on me."

Claudia even felt her fangs come out. A touch of bitter-sweet venom drip into her mouth.

"I know, I know," Vivian said, "Master like, totally said the same thing. Don't worry. I am sooo excited. I like *finally* get to go swordgal for realsie! Romeo is so going to be my first kill."

Tugging a long wavy curl in her sunny hair, Fleur gulped as tight as she tugged the hair, and it was so loud it took Vivian clearly by surprise.

"B-b-but ..." Fleur said, "Don't you ... like Romeo."

"Yeah, but ..." Vivian said, "I want him to totally die by my hand. Not our Master simply controlling usss. Isn't it totally better that way?"

"I ... guesssss," Fleur said.

Claudia liked what Vivian was thinking. Time to nudge Fleur that way too.

"Exactly," Claudia said, "So Fleur, if you really care for Romeo, and we *all* know you do, then have the guts to kill him yourself. Or at least try to. Or elssse Master Hobgobble will control us like puppets again. Like he did to kill those patrons. So painful. So agonizing. Romeo doesn't deserve that, right Fleur?"

"Yeeeah, he ..." Fleur said, "A quick death. I'll ... I'll do my bessst. Sorry I ... I hesitated. I'll—"

Vivian hugged Fleur?

"It's like totally okay," Vivian said, "Together, we'll put him down quick and painlessly. Okay?"

"Okay," Fleur said.

Claudia joined in on the hug because why not? Soon, once

the other clawgirls joined them, they all could return to Honey Heart Resort and burn that horrible place to the ground.

Feast on the dozen or so human girls there too.

Especially that bitch Tilda.

CHAPTER 12
ROMEO

Romeo knew it. The planks. They were light gray. As pale gray as the oldest patron's hair.

Not dark gray.

In other words: **dry**.

The rope too. The dry beige of faded tea leaves.

But the posts staked into the ground ... the dark brown of wet wood. There were small splatters of dark soil by their bottoms. The smell of earthy soil and mossy trees, yes, Romeo could smell that, but no musty anything from the bridge itself.

Even the smell of the river rapids below ... he could smell that. Hear the cracks and snaps of water futilely smashing boulders. The leafy curses of the bearded oaks even when the crows were cawing their brains out.

But no clinks from the bridge.

No creaks of rope stretching from the bridge.

He swore he heard the creaks before but ...

His heart thump thump thump yet he still clearly heard everything else.

Including Juliet strutting her six sexy feet toward her untimely doom.

Her stilettos squishing the soil squeally.

But no crackles from the rope.

And the cool breeze carried her scent, ah, strawberries and cream, very light, very very mild, and with a weak hint of cherries and vanilla, but ... for some reason ... unlike most of the other girls ... no, Vivian, and Fleur, and yeah, someone else, but ...

Juliet had an aroma that always carried quite aways away. It always lingered so long after she did, yet it was so mild, so gentle it never was in the slightest bit annoying, like girls who wore too much perfume, or worse, patrons who wore whole bottles of it.

Even the suggestive but subtle stretching of her bra top and miniskirt of skintight ... something ... he could hear it but not the stretch of the bridge's rope.

The wind ... wait.

The oaks were cursing in the wind. Swaying in the wind.

But the bridge wasn't swaying from the wind.

Suddenly he felt cold. Glad he always carried his harpe sword he inherited from pa. There were more than hobgobbles and clawgirls out there.

The bridge ... it should be swaying slightly.

From the wind.

But Juliet strutted between those posts not one bit

concerned. She was swaying her hips more in her well-practiced sexy strut than—

A shadow suddenly fell over everything.

A cloud in the sky?

From the corner of his sight — each and every plank — they bend a touch.

Like they were smiling.

Romeo leapt for Juliet. Grabbed her waist.

Flung her back **hard**.

(Wow, was she heavy. But he was damn strong too.)

And the bridge. It split open along its planks.

Into a saw-toothed maw.

Juliet yelped. Stumbled back.

Stopped a few steps behind the posts.

"Wha?!" she said.

"Stay back!" Romeo said and leapt in front of her.

Drew his harpe.

The bridge monster snapped at them.

CLANG!

Safe by a fraction of a hair length.

An instant later—a regular rope bridge again?!

But ... with a gash in the plank his harpe deflected.

CHAPTER 13
ROMEO

Thump thump thump, Romeo knew the thump thump thump was his heart in his ears, he was sure of it, from the nightmarish rope bridge going monster rope bridge, just like the racket behind him was the crows, and below, from the depths, the echoing roars of the water below was the foamy rapids, and the bearded oaks were the bearded oaks.

The taste in his mouth, yuck!

It was as sour and bitter as an empty stomach barely tolerating its last meal hours ago of experimental pine needle tea ...

(And not, as his pa would of reminded him over and over again, the long-forgotten taste of sweet sweet lemonade, and a sweet waste of precious sweet pennies.)

That's all.

Even now, the smells, they were just like before. Earthy

soil fresh from the recent rain. River rapids below in the canyon, smashing hopeless but persistent against the boulders.

And the bearded oaks, whispering, as if whispering planty curses in the hot wind.

Even Juliet and her ... strawberry scent.

With that lovely hint of cherries and vanilla.

(No wonder his heart was thunking so fast.)

The sinking feeling in his gut, it had to be how the rope bridge, those posts even now, how those stakes appeared so naturally grimy.

Its planks were still so naturally warped you never think it just came alive and evil hungry monster. How again this newfound bridge appeared to be here for ages.

Yes.

His thumping heart ... it all had do to with the impossible monster rope bridge here.

Like right out of a dime dreadful.

That he had almost missed that key sign — the planks were a dry light gray.

The rope too. A light beige.

And they still were.

Not dark. Not wet. Despite the recent rain.

Recent monster snap.

No cracks or creaks came from rope stretching. He swore he heard them before but ... no.

Just a brainfart. Wrong recall. That had to be it.

The bridge had no slight sway from the wind. It was perfectly still. The stray gust did nothing. The bridge monster simply hung there. It was staying far too still, too silent, like the predator it was.

That was it.

That was why his heart, thump thump thump.

Just like when a sparring match with pa got too fierce.

Yes.

Before big ma could slap some sense into her twig men and feed them heaping plates of the greasiest eggs and bacon. She always served them heaping plates, all to put some meat on them, but the only meat on them was lean and mean muscle, unlike ma, who always smelled of the kitchen she spent so much time in, but ...

The clangs of their sparing matches, the stray spark. Romeo always loved that that smell of burnt metal right afterwards.

But it was always gone as quick as it appeared too.

Yes.

That. All from that.

He never forgot that fearful thump thump of excited music from his own heart.

How to use it draw upon secret techniques.

But ... he swore he had heard cackles of rope when he first got here but ... no, still, even now, no.

Maybe he imagined it.

He trained long enough to know if you expected something hard enough, sometimes, as strange as it sounded, sometimes you'd perceived it even when it wasn't there.

That was how the most perfect of faints worked.

Not because, no, okay ... maybe, possibly, for an instant,

as she stumbled behind him, but … Juliet, her big blue beautiful eyes … but he was certain … very certain … her eyes went … serpent.

As in terrified but serpent *slitted* pupil.

Whites … less white.

A *lot* less.

A lot more gorgeously deadly blue, lightning blue, than … than …

CHAPTER 14
ROMEO

Okay okay.

For an instant, yes, Romeo knew, was sure of, Juliet's eyes really might of gone serpent for an instant, not now, now that Romeo here was just staring into nothing.

No.

The monster bridge.

First hobgobbles that ... sniiiiiff. Nope. No rotting fish. No more hobgobbles.

Then a monster bridge, which, despite the gust of heated wind, wasn't swaying or creaking still.

Now Juliet and her serpent eyes ... no.

He took a slow, caaalming breath. He savored the wind. Let it heat him. Heat away the chill down his spine.

Yes.

Just savor the exciting thump thump thump of his heart.

Let him savor it like music. Thump thump thump. A dance to be.

And savor her strawberry and cream smell.

Enjoy that hint of cherries and vanilla.

He breathed in calmly, more and more and more, let the thump thump thump become a slower thump thump thump as he breathed slow and steady for the slightest hint of serpent, but ... if she really was a clawgirl, she'd hide her serpent scent with those fruity aromas since her life depended on it.

Really.

Any of her patrons would turn her in for the bounty and the freebies Aunt Tilda would certainly end up heaping on the bastard as an apology for not vetting her girls carefully enough.

There were still bounties out on clawgirls. Good Ones. Paid in silver. More silver than Romeo could earn in a lifetime.

At least at the resort.

And those bounties that still got collected, according to patrons who did the paying, who'd insist on proof too, since murdering a random girl, a good way to get a bounty on your own neck.

But if Juliet was a clawgirl, she was a reptilian monster who imitated a gorgeous young human girl, and Juliet was the perfect example of a gorgeous human(like?) girl, but ...

Okay.

She was far from some shining good example of slavish sword fodder devoted to the overthrow of mankind, or some wicked femme fatale scheming to end humanity to avenge her sisters, no, she goofed off plenty.

Too much according to Aunt Tilda.

Like when Juliet conscripted Romeo as her oil painting subject every Wednesday morning. All because, supposedly, he could hold himself remarkably still for remarkable lengths of time, or every Tuesday, when she conscripted him for board games like Romanastia Checkers and Chess, but without the revealing toga to "set the mood" because only patrons get that, and wow, did she play so ruthlessly good she never ever let him win, not even once — for two whole years!

(Let alone leave his dignity intact.)

At least Vivian in their sword matches giggled all cutesy and taunted him plenty full of playfully teasing any guy would, well, if Vivian was some clawgirl, he's so fight her again, and as much as she wished.

And like everyone else, Romeo knew clawgirls played many seduce and slash roles in stories everywhere, but Juliet was more than practiced for the seduce.

But the slash ... as mean-spirited as she could be ...

Sigh.

A clawgirl ... would ... in fact ... make the perfect honey heart, as long as she didn't slash the patrons or anything that dumb and brutal, which Juliet wasn't dumb and ... and ... the other honey hearts ... to them ... he simply didn't exist, beyond when they needed him. Even Vivian.

Forget Fleur. She spoke all full of accented scorn at the

very thought of his presence. Not that he blamed her for it. Gotta keep up that untouchable beauty kind of appearance.

Especially around typical patrons.

Or when they needed him to fix something. Sometimes. Usually, Aunt Tilda did the asking, and the observing, not the girls.

So he had to give Juliet credit for ... that much.

Yet ... he ... deep down ... was certain. Her pupils ... they did go thin vertical slits.

From utter shock.

Slitted like a serpent. For an instant. Only an instant.

And clawgirls' lust for coin was legendary.

Just like Juliet's.

Her pale blue heart of a pouch had to be still strapped lopsided to her slim waist. It should be still heavy with the coin she earned over the years. She knew better than to let it out of her sight.

Ever.

Fleur lost so much coin from some thief, no wonder she was so scornful toward guys. Poor girl. She worked hard for that coin, and even Romeo couldn't do anything to help her there.

Even Vivian had her losses. Losses that made Aunt Tilda snatch away Vivian's blades in fear she'd slice through patrons to find the thief.

All but Juliet lost coin over the years. Some more than other.

That Juliet was gasping right behind him — okay, above

his head due to her six inches on him, and another critical strike against him in her lovely eyes.

The canyon looked so wide, and the journey to the road, so far, but climbing down, not an option, and definitely not with Juliet.

He wouldn't leave her behind, clawgirl or no.

Don't forget those hobgobbles. Who were they really after?

If Juliet was a clawgirl, was she connected to them?

According to dime dreadfuls backed by legends, hobgobbles tended to serve and obey clawgirls and do so in some weirdly devoted and fanatical way ...

Romeo made a point not to shiver. Juliet could so order hordes to doom her enemies. She was the ruthless strategist type. General-to-be kind of girl.

Nonono. He listened to his heart go thump thump thump.

Juliet was ... panting?

Definitely from shock, and a good reason too. That near death experience, maybe her first, and she sounded too girly to be a mean nasty serpent eager to die for her beloved overlords, especially if it meant slashing down more humans.

Just because every dime dreadful portrayed them that way ...

And histories he bothered to skim through ...

No.

Juliet had to be human.

He was just letting his imagination get the best of him. Pa and Uncle Jethron warned him of it. It was the opposite of letting his guard down. He'd likely do one or the other. Getting the balance right took training and experience.

And surviving long enough.

Wait.

Thump. thump. thump.

She ... wait.

He was holding her waist!

She was even letting him!

She felt so silky warm and ... slightly ... sleek. Almost like ... oiled skin, but without the wetness. A little like ... the scales of Uncle Jethro's sheath of blue clawgirl he often wore, but ... so much finer ...

Weird. The patrons would of noticed if that was how her skin normally felt. Would they? She didn't let many patrons touch her, but some did. If they paid well enough.

Juliet gulped very very loud.

"A mimic?" she said, "*Here?* But ..."

And in their human form, a clawgirl's skin was really very very very fine scales that (near) perfectly mimicked skin, but was far more protective, so ... um ... but his experience touching a young girl's skin was too limited to help.

"You okay?" Romeo said, "I ... um."

"Thanks," Juliet said, "Yes. I ... this is weird. I'm *so* sorry. I ..."

Juliet was actually apologizing to him?

Okay. He had to face her.

Settle this with his own eyes.

CHAPTER 15
ROMEO

That sudden weight of his musical heart, like back whenever Romeo starting a serious bout with his pa, no no, he was in the middle of the woods, near Shadow Forest in fact, the fringes with the big bearded oaks, the musty woods and the earthy soil fresh from the recent rains, and the river rapids smashing boulders below in the gash of a canyon.

Time to gather his courage, his strength, before the sun inched too close to sunset.

There were only a few hours of light left.

And that rumble in the distance, getting louder, the thunderstorms would strike sooner than sunset.

He also needed something more than lemonade and bitter needle tea in his stomach. He should of spent the coin for a small meal in town when he had the chance. Sure, he usually was always back by now, and would be if not for this monster rope bridge and …

Had the rope bridge monster done more than disguise itself as a bridge?

Had it muddled with distances?

Muddled his mind?

The plump crows on the branches across the canyon were still quiet and patient, as if they were waiting to be feed fresh new corpses. Were there more hobgobbles on that side of the canyon? With Juliet here, fighting them would be too dangerous.

Maybe it was best to go back to town.

The crows on this side were cawing up a storm louder than the rumbles in the distance. The echoes of thunder rumbled louder and louder through the mountains and the valleys and the passes, you'd think some mountain trolls were throwing a war party.

No.

Romeo was as strong as his blade, his harpe in his hand. It a clean and reflective. Reflect calm and …

He had to be calm and reflective.

Yes.

Calm and reflective.

This was just Juliet, after all, they were friends, in a sense, right? She did practice board games with him every week.

Every Tuesday.

She painted him in the oddest of poses and getups worthy of a dime dreadful themselves. The other honey hearts didn't even bother acknowledging his existence ever since Aunt Tilda ... well ... poor Vivian, but all the honey hearts were insanely jealous of Juliet and her gorgeous looks that ... well ...

Okay.

He was the only other young somebody she could be sort of friendly with at the inn.

And that monster rope bridge was still out there.

Right in front of them actually.

It spanned the gash of a canyon ready to munch any other foolishly naive traveler that passed this way that thought it was a lucky short-cut.

The caws behind him were bad enough.

But squint squint ... wait.

Another hint of slimy blue. Deep in the murk beyond the bearded oaks, oh ... it was gone, or ... it was just his imagination, but ... the hobgobbles before weren't.

And this rope bridge monster wasn't either.

He had underestimated it once. Nearly cost Juliet her life.

(Whether she's a clawgirl or not ...)

The sky ... there was less than a few hours of daylight left.

Not enough time to get back to the resort, but enough time to hurry back to town, if they rushed, and tomorrow morning, hurry back to the inn, using the road, and with Juliet as his witness, Aunt Tilda would believe him.

(Right?)

Juliet would understand. After seeing that bridge monster ...

She was even letting him touch her. Hold her waist even! Something only paying patrons usually got.

He *finally* ... turned to Juliet.

Kept that bout face on tight.

(But not too tight, too obvious.)

The wrong look now could give away everything in the worst possible way. How many bouts had Romeo lost to pa from his face giving away his next move ...

Too many.

Vivian was even worse. How to keep a bout face up against that gorgeous pink-haired beauty all bubbly and cutesy and amazing.

But that was practice for now, right?

Right.

And that look of utter fear on her innocent but beautiful pixie face, it still lingered on her gorgeous face, and yes, just seeing her so fearful chilled his heart like an icicle across it, in a protective manly way, but her fear didn't grow worse when he turned toward her ... which oddly comforted him some.

Looking deep up into her eyes and ...

Holy Mother of the Flame Moon ... big, blue, and *gorgeous* **serpent** eyes.

No wonder she always smelled so sweetly of strawberries and cream. That hint of cherries and vanilla. He'd read so many dime dreadfuls yet never put one and one together ...

Clawgirls always smelled so naturally fruity, in a sweet and mild way, according to every dime dreadful ever. It was one of their innate beauty magics, including the one that helped them stay on the clean side, to up their seductress skills.

Ugh.

His heart felt like an icicle went right through it but ... he best keep his best bout face on.

(No telling how'd she react if he blurted it out.)

So Romeo smiled warmly. As warm as the wind blowing her waist-long sunny hair.

The complete opposite of his chilly insides.

"You never apologized to me before now," he said, "Apology accepted."

"You never deserved it before now," she said and smiled slightly more.

(Those strawberry red lips never looked so kissable ... until now.)

(Okay, she wasn't usually nice to him at all, but ... even if she was a clawgirl ...)

"Ouch," he said, "Just when I thought you'd finally be nice—"

"Don't get the wrong idea," she said, "My virginity auction starts tomorrow and the bids will be more silver than you could ever earn in ... you know."

(Okay, she *was* a clawgirl, and clearly didn't realize her eyeball oopsie, yet, but ...)

(But that war between humans and monsters was centuries ago. Over a thousand years ago. Juliet was eighteen today. So well before her time and his. Tomorrow she was no longer too young to sleep with the patrons, although Aunt Tilda did say Romeo could marry any of the girls free of charge if he won any of them over but until now ... even Vivian seemed too ... distant. Forget a girl like Fleur, let alone Juliet. They all were marriage-aged now and "unsoiled" and like she said, that virginity auction ... too late for Vivian and Fleur but Juliet ... he was already a good solid twenty something and ...)

((If she were human.))

(Well ... if she were human and not a honey heart. Even a human Honey Heart wasn't exactly angling for marriage except to the richest of the richest.)

But ... come to think of it, those ancient baelzog overlords were long dead and dust. Beyond dust. They had to be. No reports of them except out of dime dreadfuls. Just because there was still a bounty on the heads of all their monster minions ... a relic from ancient times.

Yes. A relic.

(Probably.)

((But the harpe in his other hand, a bit of a relief, just in case those lovely slim hands go talons for his throat.))

Why she was looking down ... while Romeo um ...

Juliet gulped.

Whispered.

Raised her hands to her cheeks, brushing right under her big blue serpent eyes and ...

"That sword ..." she said, "M-my ... eyes ... no ..."

Her skin changed to gorgeous serpent scales so bubblegum bright and exotically pink they'd be worth more than any honey heart virginity auction result.

Maybe even a few goldies.

Especially those lip scales. Juicy bright strawberry red.

Her nails, they had become such gorgeously bright red like her lips. Razor eagle-like claws. One that ... each big talon would certainly be worth a good few silvers on top of her the many many coins for the rest of her.

Never mind that her sunny hair was really scales. Incredibly strong and silky fine scales ... and quite valuable in themselves, especially for such a gorgeous golden blonde color.

Not that he intended to collect but ... better idea forming. Now. Chance of a lifetime and ...

Romeo smiled gently. "So you're a clawgirl—"

"YESSSSSSS!" she said and dashed off into the woods so quick ...

She had startled him enough that ... she could of killed him dead just as quick—if she wanted to.

But no.

She panicked. Ran.

Ran right into danger.

The deadly dangers of Shadow Forest.

He knew exactly what to do now.

He dashed off after her. To rescue her.

CHAPTER 16
JULIET

Juliet just knew she was *sooo* stupid stupid stupid she shouldn't of played human for so long and now she had to run run run run run and in high stiletto heels of all things but somehow she did know how to run *fast* in heels and she had **long** killer legs and this heart-themed bikini outfit was real easy to run in and only ferns slapped her legs like all those old creepy men eager for more but not until ...

Nononono — not *ever* now.

She was six feet tall but she never fought a day in her life. Really. Okay, since she got mistaken for a human.

Her life before that didn't count.

(Right?)

She avoided the topic as much as the other honey hearts avoided her, but now ... her heart raced faster than her legs and the smell ...

She was huffing and huffing and huffing and only smelled, tasted earthy soil like the gardens she tended in front of her room that ... no.

She'd never return to now ...

Must never return to.

The musty oaks and their moss ... it only reminded her of the days so long ago. How often she napped in moss beds, back when she was just one of many clawgirl kiddies ... called wormlings being raised for that day of stupid stupid vengeance over things dead and gone but ... if only ...

(Chosen of the Flame ... yeah. Right.)

In her human form ... she had looked enough like a real human teen that she eventually got mistaken for one and lucky her, ended up at the Honey Heart Resort.

She *so* remembered the smell of the crows that loved to follow her pack as a wormling. Their incessant caws and they loved to feast on the leftover corpses that she, with her many sisters, took down and ...

Would her sisters even welcome her back?

Well ... she'd need to find them first. Where ... where were they? She never had the chance to contact them. Those creepy men who paid bounties to hunters who killed her kind never spoke much of it, but they did mention the rare bounty paid out.

Nothing on a pack of clawgirls.

Not even a rumor.

Back when she was in her pack, there was usually plenty for everyone and as long as you did your share you got a decent share but slackers got less and only slackers.

The gamey taste of squirrels—yuck—but they made a decent stew and bunnies she used to love to roast but yuck if she mistook a hare for a bunny and bang bang the others would smack her head if she got the two mixed up but, well, until she got adopted by humans, by pure lucky mistake, and learned the wonders of real food and ...

She didn't forget how to cook, no, but she didn't expect to be used as a cook, not by the humans who wanted other things from her, but ...

Okay.

The way to a man's heart can (sometimes) be through his stomach, and cooking did remind her of the days she didn't have to pretend to be human and her sisters loved her cooking, and wow, was there plenty of fallen branches she could use for tinder.

Plenty of fallen leaves.

They even softened her footsteps.

And they would hide her trail—if not for her heels poking holes through each and every one of them.

Bears and wolves loved trying to munch her and her sisters back when they were little wormlings, but if a wormling shifted in time to her scaled form, the beasts' fangs broke when they tried to bite.

But it still hurt plenty.

The bites had left her skin scales marred bad until she molted and if only she hadn't just molted an hour ago.

It was the only reason she took this long cut through the middle of nowhere.

Concentrate. Focus.

She'd survive this.

Romeo was no doubt chasing her for the huuuuuge bounty he'd earn killing her. Selling her body parts to patrons. To other creeps.

That weird blade of his ... she refused to shutter.

She was a clawgirl. It was her duty to survive.

Fight him to the death ... if need be.

Her first fight ... with a human ...

But she hadn't run like this in ages. It's only a matter of time before she winded herself, gave Romeo an easy kill.

No.

Ambush him.

Yesssss.

CHAPTER 17
JAGGER

Hanging off his blade, Jagger gazed deep in the churning depths, among that foamy water, sniii-iffff, yes, there, caught between the boulder right below him and the rocky cliff, deep in the foam, that hint of pink was no illusion, no trick of the light.

It was the molted scales of a clawgirl.

And sniiffff. Just to be sure.

A hint of serpent.

Clawgirl.

Serpent with ... with ... strawberries and cream ... sniiiffff ... with ... yess ... it wasn't from the cliff but from below, that a hint of cherries and vanilla too.

All the same smells of that girl that passed by.

Except serpent.

But clawgirls only stunk of serpent when they molted,

and only their old skin stunk of serpent, and only after some time had passed.

No doubt the clawgirl had come this way to molt in secret.

Against a lesser ranger, one without Bloodhound Nose, this canyon would of easily hidden her scales. The waters below would of washed them far away.

Through Shadow Forest and beyond.

The rumbles in the distance, thunderstorms were coming. The coming rain would wash away most of the scent trails, but not enough to lose him.

Only slow him down.

Judging by the scent of her outfit ... how expensive it must be ... she must be one of the girls from that Honey Heart Resort. A clever hiding spot.

But not clever enough.

He was the Marque of the Black Hound Clan. His nose was enough to kill the girl outright.

Or imprison her.

Depending on her temperament.

He knew of Honey Heart Resort. Right now she was a slave with a high price tag. Buying her ... no, it would soil the reputation of his clan.

An exotic clawgirl ... such a high bounty ... and sniiifff, yes, that sour hint of day-to-day terror from a secret that must never be revealed.

He smelled how young she was.

Jagger grimaced.

Gathered himself back onto the edge. Stood back up.

He had dealt with such creatures before. Clawgirls only looked like beautifully dumb bimbos. They were often smarter than they looked. Those who weren't rarely lived long enough to matter. And they often picked up far more information than their dragotroll masters preferred. That was the reason their masters often bound them so forcefully. That compulsion to obey was a dark magic and far more limited than what most realized, but only because of the effort it took maintain the bond, to compel orders per slaved clawgirl.

So, in truth, killing her outright, even if she revealed herself right away, no, she might have important information, and if she was still free ...

Hmmm.

He curled his goatee. Looked up into the sky.

A storm was coming soon.

The rumble of thunder, not so distant.

And such an exotic clawgirl in such a remote location ... strange.

Exotic clawgirl were known for their rare but useful powers. It's a major reason why they fetched such high bounties. Not only were they find ingredients for magical items, they were one less important piece for the enemies of humanity.

But Jagger did more than learn smells over the years.

So he knew training clawgirls right took time and resources. Some of their skills, of course, were innate, but less so than what most thought. That the few dragotrolls who wasted their clawgirls never lasted long.

But the Honey Heart Resort, from what he knew of it, no

clawgirl could never use her power there, let alone practice it without risk of discovery.

He stepped back from the canyon.

Smelled the trails by the cliff.

Hmmmm.

Such a luxurious life this clawgirl must be living there. Pleasuring a few filthy men, a small price to pay for luxury she could never hope to otherwise obtain.

And despite the silly tales called dime dreadfuls, some of his clawgirl quarries were just simply clawgirls mistaken as young human girls at some point, and the lucky clawgirl simply went along with it, enjoyed the life of a human girl while she could, simply hoping never to be caught, until she was.

By him.

But their information was always limited.

Outdated.

So far the King secretly conscriped those clawgirls. A pardon in exchange for some secret duties, and Jagger often helped in those duties. He didn't need to see the reports to know their help had drastically reduced the troubles with hobgobbles over the years.

But none of those clawgirls had been exotics.

Bringing in an exotic clawgirl to the King ... caution. If the prophecies were true ... no, destiny was never so simple.

But, at first, some of those pardoned clawgirls had gotten bound forcefully by their original masters. Compelled to betray their new duties and serve as proper clawgirls against humanity.

Until the King arranged all pardoned clawgirls to be bound as familiars to warriors. His magicians constructed a similar but different bond. One far less one-sided than the ones the clawgirls' original master would bind them with.

Not that Jagger ever accepted a request by any clawgirl to become his familiar.

Yet.

But the King sending Jagger to root out so many clawgirls, only for the King to spare most of them, no, Jagger knew the King knew plenty more were still hidden among the populace, and neither were fools.

Bring her to the King and let him decide her fate.

CHAPTER 18
JULIET

Juliet ran ran ran.

Long killer legs made her quick quick quick.

Her stilettos sly daggers.

Her talons even better daggers. Whatever power they had ... hopefully a good one.

(Maybe.)

And the thrill of the hunt sugared her veins like like, but the fear of injury, of actually dying made her want to shutter but nonononono.

She zigzagged through the big trees. Avoided the slippery moss.

The trunks of the big trees were wider than her bed, and in fact, her bed was made from a slice of their trunk's base.

(How she'd miss a real bed soon enough! Damn Romeo!)

(Yes! *Hate* your enemy. **Hate** him. He planned to kill her so get raging ready to kill him first. Yes. *Raging* ready. What clawgirls like her were renown for. Go full dime dreadful clawgirl.)

(But ... weren't they friends? She played with him every Tuesday — for free, even. Painted him every Wednesday. All that free honey heart time with him and and and no other girl there noticed him except to fix stuff they needed fixed or even that slut Vivian except when she was forced to spar with him.)

(Humphf. Figures. *Men.*)

The moss on her bed back at the resort was preserved and enhanced with alchemy but too many bugs loved to hide in it and nononononononono but ...

Eating bugs again ... yesssss.

She'd have to.

For now.

They weren't ... so bad ... when roasted right. Maybe she'd get to fry them, if she found the right shroom to oil.

She was free too.

Unlike her sisters years ago. They were stuck serving that dragotroll bastard but ever since Juliet was mistake for one of the little girl prisoners back—wait.

Free?!

But her virginity auction ... so much coin ... more silver than she could hope to earn in any other way ... even if Boss Tilda kept plenty of it, Juliet would of gotten ... no, now her auction would never happen and ...

Okay. Honestly, it was like a boulder off her shoulders.

No.

A **mountain.**

And there were plenty of mountains in this place.

Way too many mountains. You'd think there'd be more hobgobbles in these parts.

If only there were any around here. She would so enlist them to wear down Romeo.

And hobgobbles were always willing to serve a clawgirl.

Perk of being a clawgirl. Her wormling sisters found it so easy to enlist the stray hobgobble to help them out it was ridiculous.

The other honey hearts would be amazed how well Juliet could run despite the size of her chest, but human girls, as she discovered, didn't have supportive muscles there. They were always so jealous of Juliet and her looks and, now, ever since that prince rejected her she worked so hard on her brains too but now ...

Wow.

This bra, with its big heart cups, it was *amazingly* supportive, and this outfit itself, the miniskirt was like a heart-themed loincloth but better since the thin vanilla straps over the side of her thighs also prevented the upside-down hearts from flapping and revealing too much underneath ...

Wow, did Boss Tilda make sure the material of these getups stretch well and cozy, right up to revealing.

But magic ensured they resisted the right limit *hard*.

All in all, a girl, with a little skill and practice, only revealed her best goods only when she meant to.

(Even Vivian with her ridiculous flips and flops during

her sword fights that she always let patrons always win—or else.)

But best of all, human girls with such big chests would struggle painfully to run so fast, but a clawgirl, he-he, nope.

Juliet grimaced. "Honey Horror time."

Yeah.

Proud.

Go all clever quippy. Romeo loved those dime dreadfuls. He loved when Vivian did it during those awful bouts. If stuffy Fleur had ever managed it, wow, she might actually of surpassed Juliet, but phew, that blondie was too stiff and sure of herself.

Enough patrons read those dime dreadfuls too that all the girls there read plenty of them. Knew to reference them at the right moments. And how many clawgirls in them had crazy amazing claw powers and always cracked a clever wicked quip at the right moment.

Sigh.

If only she could be so awesome.

No. She will be. Yup.

She smirked. Flexed her talons. Free ... to do what she really wanted ...

First focus on what's ahead. A strategy. Don't act like some brainless bimbo. Just play one.

Don't be one.

Ever.

She zigzagged more and more. Don't make the trail too obvious. Too easy. Make Romeo work to find her.

She turned faster than any mere human girl.

Go random.

Throw him off some. She always won all their games.

This should be easy.

Yesss. Pay attention to the trees. Watch for good ambush spots, but don't choose anything too obvious. Maybe ... hope beyond hope Romeo wouldn't even catch up.

Okay. He definitely would.

But hopefully not too soon.

Her fangs ... they were ready, no, eager for boy blood.

(If she needed them.)

Bite him and her venom would slave him plenty. Along long as she nipped him enough. Even snakes couldn't kill with their bites all the time. Not that clawgirls were snakes but ... just thinking of biting his tasty sweet flesh ... shutter no!

Stumble nono stumble **no** CRASH!

Right into a big stupid tree.

Owie owie owie.

(Stupid her.)

The moss ... the only reason she didn't break any bones. Her skin. Her precious perfect skin scales were ...

Her legs, her tummy, her arms ... all still pretty pink.

Not a scratch?

Phew.

Oh. Yeah.

In this form ... her scales ... they were *really* protective. It took a **really** sharp blade to pierce them but ... Romeo's blade looked sharp enough and it did damage that bridge mimic and ... she didn't want to test out her scales ... or her talons on him.

Unless she had to.

Her talons power ... or powers ... only mature clawgirls had real talon powers—oh yeah, she was mature enough. She was eighteen today. An adult. Young but an adult. No crying for kiddie mercy anymore. A few more years and she could bare wormlings too and ...

Nononononono.

(No way she could raise wormlings on her own.)

(Think Juliet think.)

All adult clawgirls could throw their slashes like flying wind slashes. If only she had time to figure out how. The dime dreadfuls didn't exactly detail that out.

And no instruction manuals for going clawgirl.

No one to ask.

Least the dime dreadfuls didn't exaggerate that bit. Well, for experienced clawgirls. They could easily make armored knights explode with their flying slashes. Her clawgirl ability, whatever it was, would go with her bright pink scales, and and and ... that rumble in the distance ...

What was her power ... time to find out.

No. Soon. Not now.

It was too dangerous to practice them before but now ... once she had time ... once she dealt with Romeo ...

She knew she was worth more than a few silvers on looks alone. Pink scales? Exotic clawgirl. Lots of coin. Throw in her looks ... she was worth ... goldies at this point, especially if her talons had the right power.

Too many goldies for that creep to pass up.

She bared her fangs at the thought. After being so nice to him … well, compared to the other honey hearts … and she hadn't shown her fangs in … showed her beautiful pink scales … she didn't want to die but … then …

Romeo had to die.

(Sorry Romeo.)

((Stupid creep.))

Boss Tilda might suspect but … no. If Romeo died Juliet could return and … nononononono.

Boss Tilda would suspect something, and that big woman was persistent and so determined to protect her dear little Romeo that … nonononono.

Even Vivian couldn't get close to that creep. Win herself a debt jubilee *and* a matching idiot for a hubby that … no.

Focussss.

Maybe. Avoid killing Romeo but … how …

Juliet wasn't … she never … actually … killed a human before.

Her sisters did. Plenty of times. Juliet … helped them … but never landed an actual blow.

Yet.

She helped cooked the bodies, of course, but never really helped kill one.

Forget actually fighting one.

Her first strike against humanity … as much as she didn't want … no.

She was a clawgirl. If peace were an option then … no.

No peace while the bounties were in place.

If peace were an option, then bounties would be for what she did, not what she was. Humans want war as much as that dragotroll and its ... whatevers ...

Gulp.

She wasn't a weak and helpless human girl like Fleur against any spider no matter how itty bitty, no, Juliet could handle this.

Yessssss.

So what if her hunting skills were soooo out of practice?

Practice made perfect and Romeo was the perfect practice.

(Then she'd find a pack of clawgirls and ... maybe a different name, so none of that Chosen nonsense. No telling if humans heard of it what crazy bounty stuff they'd put on her assss.)

This tree she ran into ... wow. It had a massive huge hole she just missed running into.

Phew.

(Imagine getting stuck and ... nononono. Horrible, *embarrassing* way to ...)

That would of been real painful. Maybe mar her scales painful. The hole was like a gash that she could easily slip into for cover tonight, and wait, if she slipped in just right and—

SCREEEEECH!

CHAPTER 19
ROMEO

The bearded oaks hid the source of the screech, but Romeo didn't hesitate. Pa never did. Ma neither.

This wasn't another fun bout with Vivian either.

Harpe in hand Romeo dashed faster.

And faster.

Torn through the ferns.

Hoping beyond hope he'd reach Juliet in time.

The smell ferns ripping, as crisp the sound, and it spiked his determination. Kept his heart racing steady.

The soil, so earthy dark, like the smell, but those many many leaves, her stilettos left such a distinct trail, but kudos to Juliet for such speed and amazing zigzagging in high heels. That took *skill*.

If he were after her for the bounty ... wow, she might of escaped, except ... no. That screech ...

No hope she'd outrace whatever monster screeched ahead.

Good thing he wore slacks. His slacks deflected the whips of the ferns. His loose vest didn't slow him down at all.

And the screech was so loud it silenced the crows.

Smothered the planty whispers of the trees.

(If only Juliet could summon some hobgobbles to ... no. No that was asking for serious trouble—

Ah!

He was already stepping only on wet silent leaves like his pa smacked into him. Back during his training, pa chucked a stone at him whenever he stepped on a loud leaf and trying to dodge one of those stones ...

Romeo smirked at how well his training had already kicked in.

The shadows were like the molasses ma one time spilled everywhere in the kitchen when her one and only massive jar of it shattered.

And the smell here was so earthy yet so musty it was like that time, back at the inn, he fell head first through a wide-open window and into the garden in front of Juliet's room, back when he was repairing that very wide-open window.

No.

Focus.

He refused to pant. Refused let the smell burn his tongue.

Focus.

Every bout with Vivian required being in topmost shape. A single sign of fatigue and he was a goner.

And this was even more important.

He had to breathe deep, quick, but not too quick. It pricked his insides good, but not enough to slow him. The cool air was refreshing. It gave him that edge no handy work ever could. Upped his speed.

As pa taught him.

His heart thump thump thumping.

A thump per step.

Good. Rhythm to fight with.

And no Vivian singing jiggles to distract him either.

His suede boots let him feel how soggy the ground was, how each step squished the soil, since it was soft, very moist from the rain earlier, but not sticky mud goo, only because of the many many ferns rooting it together, and the many bearded oaks.

Yet he could feel each and every pebble.

Each pebble was buried so very shallow, so very sharp here, yet their smooth pricks, he refused to yelp for a single one of them.

The slippery feel of the ground, it let him adjust instantly, like all those times he raced over huge slippery boulders after a downpour.

Avoid sliding.

Avoid losing critical moments.

Another screech!

Up right ahead! Passed these last two bearded oaks and ...

CHAPTER 20
CLAUDIA

At that awfully loud screech, one that shook the whole forest, rattling it and Claudia to her core. She froze perfectly.

Reptilian perfect frozen.

The screech came from in front of them. Only dozens of paces away. The steaming hot wind already blew the scent of that tasty but sweaty boy musk of Romeo their way. That strange crack, and the strangely friendly chit chat between Juliet and Romeo ...

No.

Not Romeo. The target. He had been around this last curve of the canyon. On the very same path between the forest and the canyon. Headed toward them, not away, as they all had clearly thought.

But a shortcut through the woods was blocked by a

natural barrier of boulders and gigantic trees. All full of murky slippery moss.

How could they lose him when he was so clossse?

And when Claudia was leading the way … Master Hobgobble might punish her … no, that's if they really do lose him.

Behind her, Claudia checked and good, Fleur and Vivian had both frozen too, but their gaze was following the sounds of dashing away.

Vivian whispered. "We need to save Juliet."

Fleur gulped. "Yeah. I'll … f-f-feather him. If he … hurts her."

Claudia growled. "*When* he hurts her, it'll be too late. Come on. They're not far."

But moving her body, harder than she imagined?

"Wait for me, he-he."

That whiny know-it-all voice … coming up behind them.

"Vanessa?" Claudia said, "You're a …"

"Clawgirl extraordinaire," Vanessa said, "Like you all. Don't worry. I'm the last of the lot here at this resort. Besides Juliet there."

Vanessa strutted right in front of Claudia. Even taller than Claudia, she looked down at all three of them. Her dark brown gaze like a quagmire of serpent slitted doom.

Claudia barely managed to gasp.

"A paralysis power?" she said, "On ussss?"

That long-haired brunette giggled again. In a green version of their clawgirl garb. It even looked good against her tanned dark skin. Skin scales actually.

"Of course, silly," Vanessa said, "we need to know who's boss. Queen bee of our little hive. Princess of the pack."

Fleur actually managed to gasp.

"Juliet," Fleur said. "needs. our. help."

Vivian tsked. "Claudia please. Not now."

"Me?" Claudia said, "I'm not. freezing. us."

"Exactly," Vanessa said, "The princess is the most powerful and who's the most powerful here? Anyone want to guesss?"

Silence.

Except for another awful terrible screech nearby.

Claudia growled. "You are, Princess Vanessa."

"Princess Vanessa," Fleur and Vivian said together.

"Good," Vanessa said, "and we're going to set some things clear, right?"

Silence?

Oh no.

"Right," Claudia said.

Vanessa glared cold and angry.

"Together or ..." Vanessa said, and snapped her fingers and then her eyes ...

Ouch ouch ouch ouch. Claudia. Her whole body. Like it. Needles all over. yet couldn't move.

When the pain vanished.

"There's no 'i' in team, right clawgals?" Vanessa said.

"Right!" all three clawgirls said together.

"Juliet's only worth rescuing," Vanessa said, "if she's able to hold off Romeo for a bit, while we do what Master Hobgobble needs ussss to do ... nearby."

After listening Claudia ... gulped. Her body feeling even colder, more awful than ... but like Vivian said, better do it herself than as a puppet that then would be broken afterwards and and and—

Vanessa giggled again.

"Romeo must die," she said, "and no quick nice death for him. Unless Juliet does her job right for once and finishes him before we recruit her properly. Since we need Master Hobgobble for that part and he's ... busy, but not for long. Once we free that dragotroll ... he-he. Romeo better be long dead and Honey Heart Resort the next meal on the menu, right clawgals?"

Silence? Oh no ...

"Right!" Claudia said.

"Right!" Fleur and Vivian said almost with her.

Almost.

"Ooooh nooooes," Vanessa said, "it looks like you three first need some training. Painful training. To get the wimp and the hesitation out of you three. Make you proper blood-thristy clawgals, am I right?"

None of you clawgurls have earned the right to call yourself Princess of anything.

They all gasped. But Claudia was the one who spoke.

"Master Hobgobble?" she said.

From behind them all another girl spoke out.

"Master Hobgobble knows all," the new girl said, "Master Hobgobble was busy claiming me from my patrons. Like he did with all of you."

Claudia turned and ...

CHAPTER 21
ROMEO

A clearing?

Yes! Romeo found a small clearing!

A round clearing. No bearded oaks—except one.

A huge one right in the center.

The smell of fresh moist soil. And strawberries.

With a hint of cherries.

Good. Juliet.

The ground was flat. A mix of dark moist soil and half-buried boulders jutting out of it. The rock was gray and smooth like the buried mace traps Uncle Jethro loved to set up against smaller monster menaces.

But the clearing was all shaded dark by a massive huge bearded oak right in the center.

A massive gash of a hole in the oak, and ah!

Juliet was inside.

As a beautifully pink clawgirl. Still in her blue heart bikini-wear.

Good.

But two massive birds were attacking the hole ...

No.

Her.

The birds looked like blue jays. Blue jays the size of stallions.

No. Not blue jays.

Jumping raptors.

Their smell ... like overgrown caged birds with the savage stink of predators eager for tasty girl prey.

They screeched again. Songbird style but so, so loud.

Only a dozen feet away their cries speared his ears.

But that was nothing compared to the pain he'd inflict on them.

Quiet as a falling feather. Quick as a hangry wasp. Romeo darted up behind them.

Like a cougar.

Leapt at the closest.

But kept his harpe way down. Razor-side up.

Falling he grabbed its wing. Shoved his weight into it.

The jumping raptor shrieked.

Shocked.

Jerked down. Away. All by instinct.

Toward his unseen blade.

He sliced up. Slit deep into its neck.

Gurgling blood it toppled over.

Another hungry screech — and worse to come.

CHAPTER 22
ROMEO

The screech was so loud the whole forest and then some must of heard it.

Even the overexcited crows stopped cawing again.

(Definitely hoping for some leftovers.)

The huge bearded oak and its big crack still hid Juliet, but it wasn't enough to slow the other jumping raptor.

No.

The smell of fresh gusting blood only excited it.

And the jumping raptor, that overgrown blue jay, it perched tight on a stubby ledge of rock near the tree. Wings out to balance itself. Its talons so big they could easily crack open a man's skull.

And as tall as Juliet was, that ledge gave the jumping raptor a good height advantage over her.

But with her claws Juliet had somehow managed to grab that raptor's beak.

Hold it back.

(For now.)

((Clawgirls did have some good strength, after all.))

But her grimace. Even with her pink scales and beautifully strawberry red lips, Romeo knew even in her serpent form, Juliet wasn't strong enough to stop the jumping raptor for long. With all her strength she was only slowing the monster down.

It still reached. Pushed back against her grip.

Slow.

Steady.

Snap snapping hangry for her pretty face.

Too intent to notice Romeo silently marching right up to it.

Till Juliet looked his way shocked and terrified. As if she were the one he came to kill.

She cried. "No! Please! We're friends, right? I-I-I."

"Good friends," Romeo said and ducked just in time.

Just as the bird flapped its massive wing at his skull.

Ruffled his untamed hair instead.

He rolled under the wing. Up to his feet.

It stomped at him. Its talons almost racking his gut.

Almost.

He dodged backwards.

Slashing around. At its head.

It flinched.

But Juliet's gripe spelled its doom.

It couldn't dodge Romeo hooking it through the eye.

Into its brain.

It collapsed instantly.

Romeo cleaned his harpe with its feathers. He had no rag so why not? Better than letting the blood dry on the blade.

"Now Juliet," Romeo said and smiled friendly.

Juliet raised her claws. "Please ... I-I-I surrender. Please ... I ..."

Romeo sighed. Didn't know what to say. What would pa say to ma if ... but ma wasn't obsessed with gold, but Uncle Jethron to ... no, wait.

That's it!

CHAPTER 23
CLAUDIA

Claudia was shocked again. Enough that her thirst for boy blood was ... lessened.

The louder rumble of thunder in the not-so distant distance couldn't be complete coincidence either.

Because on the slim path between the canyon and the forest, the very path Claudia and the other clawgirls here all traveled down in clawgirl archer outfits even, coming around the curve behind the thick craggy oaks and the bracken ... Claudia tried her best not to gasp.

Let her heart race too fast.

Behind Fleur and Vivian, that blue-haired witch Melissa. Curly sky-blue hair framing a heart of a droopy always depressed face that always sent patrons scrambling to throw more coin at her.

Not that her gorgeous hourglass physique didn't elicit as

much concern, despite her breasts only being D-cup and her heart-themed slutwear was only as blue as her hair.

Her slim hands were in talon form.

Her archer outfit was as blue as her hair, as blue as Fleur's was.

Worse. An icicle was pointed sharp end first right at Fleur's heart. At Vivian's heart.

Even at Claudia's and Vanessa's heart.

Fleur gasped. "You're ... a clawgirl too?"

Vivian sighed. Stroked her rosy pink hair.

"How silly of us," Vivian said, "No secret is safe from that hobgobble, am I right?"

RIIIIPPPPP!

Their leotards. Their own hands had turned taloned. Clawed. Hand ripped a square gap neat and trim. By their own claws. Controlled by Master Hobgobble.

Now their upper bosom was exposed?

Their icicles slipped snug between their breasts. Chilling their bosom painfully. The tip jagging just slightly the scales in front of their heart.

And this was death that even Claudia, who didn't read every single dime dreadful, knew wouldn't come quick, but it sure would be awful and painful. All the girls knew it. From the dime dreadfuls. For their patron's amusement when they understood the books ridiculous references. Nothing more.

But as serpents, their bodies would live on long enough that Master could use them as puppets as they died slowly and painfully from being staked through the heart.

Claudia couldn't even move. Same, no doubt, for the other clawgirls.

Except Vanessa somehow managed to gnash her teeth loudly at Vivian's tease. Too defiantly that their master was sure to punish them all even more later.

"Right, Vivian," Melissa said, "Including your own. If you consider hesitating again. If you even humor letting that boy harm you, waste Master's effort in claiming you, in claiming any of usss, rather than ending him as Master wishes ..."

Vivian gulped. Loud. Her long lush pink hair framed how much fear radiated from that cute face of hers.

Vivian curtsied. "I ... understand."

Her icicle evaporated? Bottom first. No ... something was off. The tension in her face.

"And Fleur," Melissa said, "Same for you. Stammering is one thing. Hesitating is another. You better understand the difference. Master watches ussss in body and mind. There are no secrets from Master. *Ever.*"

Fleur eeped. "I do, I do."

She curtsied too. And her icicle evaporated into her chest but ...

"I'm as expandable as all of you," Melissa said, "But Master put effort into collecting usss. Just like he intends to collect Juliet. Our Honey Heart training will prove far too useful for later plans to die here, but ... if we can't take down a single pathetic boy ... Master's disappointment ..."

Melissa clearly cringed. Was even more depressed. Her icicle evaporating was clearly not the relief it should of been.

Claudia nodded. The pain of her next words ... but they had to be said. Acknowledged.

"We all understand," Claudia said, "We exist to serve Master Hobgobble. Nothing more."

Claudia's icicle didn't evaporate?

"Exactly," Melissa said, "Even if it means killing your sister Fleur for daring to defy our massster once again, understand?"

"I ..." Claudia said, "understand. Better she die by my own hands than Master's."

And those words, not a lie or deception. As much as they hurt to say. To accept.

Claudia's icicle evaporated from the bottom to ... no.

A sliver of the point remained buried snug in her bosom. More than enough to kill her painfully and slowly. Let Master control her body as a puppet even better.

Fleur froze. Reptilian perfectly.

Then suddenly her body went into motion. Like a puppet. She split her bow in half. Into two wicked bone scimitars.

The blades a hair's widths from her own neck.

Only her wide blue eyes remained in her sister's control.

"I-I-I understand," Fleur said, "Better by my sister's hands than ... Master's"

She gulped. "I won't hesitate. Not a-a-anymore."

None of them would.

Or elsssse.

CHAPTER 24
ROMEO

Heart thumping music, but Romeo knew this wasn't a battle.

Far from it. Romeo had to be wiser than the old guys those bearded oaks resembled. Despite the earth musty smell of the forest, this close up to Juliet, her strawberry and cream scent ... no no, distracting and too heart thumping, no.

The wind heated the moment hotter than ... than ... and the trees whispered, no cheered him on.

Gulp.

The shadows didn't keep the place cool enough. The stone he stood on, his boots couldn't protect him from the hot rock.

Still, he read enough about clawgirls. In dime dreadfuls and in the stray history he brought over to the inn. He overheard plenty from enough patrons to confirm what's true and what's not.

So no way Juliet would truly believe Romeo would forego the hefty bounty of her lovely head, not without something in return.

Good. In a way. Few guys should be trusted anyway.

Especially in this situation.

Least he figured out what to say.

"Your bounty," he said, "With that golden hair and those gorgeously exotic pink scales, wow, it'll be a good amount over your virgin price."

"Yeah," she said and gulped.

Shuttered. Good, she had no delusions about that.

"I ..." Romeo said and gulped himself.

She shut her eyes tight. "Make it quick."

She even cringed so adorably tight he almost shuttered.

Almost.

He brushed her side with his fingertips and wow, were her scale so sleek and silky, and warm, he never touched anything like them, yet they so so warm, they made ma's fresh made pudding seem like cool sour ... stuff.

Yes.

Stuff.

Except, she tensed so much under his touch ...

"How about a deal?" he said.

"A ... deal?" she said and somehow cringed even more.

Damn, he almost felt like the bad guy here, and he wasn't intending on taking advantage of her, not really, let alone hurting her.

"Instead of collecting your bounty," he said, "I get your hand in marriage, and you count that nice sweet bounty of goldies I didn't collect toward—"

Juliet gasped. "OKAY!"

She held her claws clenched together. Over her stunning chest.

A chest that, despite her pink scales and her bright red talons, it was still a guy's dream come true, and at eye level with him, and he knew he had no hope of snagging a better girl, looks or ... you know.

Romeo met her eyes again. They were so wide big and intensely blue. Like the zircon gems some of the patrons gifted her with, and no doubt were stuffed inside her pouch.

"Your eyes are gorgeous," he said and sheathed his harpe.

She didn't even try attacking him.

As he thought. She had her chance back at the bridge. She wasn't that sort of girl, clawgirl or not.

So he offered his hand to her.

"This serpent side of you is ..." he said, "Exotic ... in a good way."

"You ... trust me?" Juliet said, "I ... I never thought ..."

They were friends, after all, so ...

"Back at the bridge," he said, "You could of killed me, but you didn't. You ran for your life. That's ... not exactly the behavior of a clawgirl out to slaughter mankind."

"Well ... yeah, I never ..." she said, "You ... would you believe I never actually really well ... hurt a human ... before. Not really. I ..."

"Sure," he said, "I bet as a kid, your pack had you do other things. Maybe awkward to speak about now but ... you've never said anything about your life before you arrived at Honey Heart Resort."

"You ... didn't ask," she said and nervously accepted his hand by resting her fisted talons on his palm.

More kudos in her favor.

She recognized how dangerous her talons were in this form and knew to be careful.

"I didn't want to pry," he said, "I was hoping you'd tell me when you were ready, but now we're agreed to marry ..."

"Ooo," Juliet said, "Yeah. Sorry."

She hopped out of the bearded oak.

"I'm ... still ... shocked you ..." she said and gulped.

"Asked to marry you," he said, "Instead of, you know."

She grimaced. Kissed his forehead.

"Yeah, and ..." she said, "My bounty ... no other guy I know would pass it up to ... you know. More like maybe fuck me for a while then when they're tired of me, turn me in for the bounty."

"True," he said, "Lucky for us I was the one to discover your secret."

"Lucky ..." she said, "And ..."

She gulped, but smiled. "Time for you to get even luckier."

CHAPTER 25
JAGGER

Jagger couldn't help but hesitate at the sight of that rope bridge.

The graying sky above didn't help either. It smelled of rain.

Severe rain.

But the rope smelled of musty rope and wood. Too much so. There were no other scents coming off the bridge. No beast or bird and most rope bridges had a few rodent smells. Sometimes some birds too.

At the very least, some of their refuse.

The stakes smelled too earthy dark as well. No sign of rodents underneath the soil by them.

His eyes did not miss the sword slash in one of the planks, and his nose smelled the zesty zing only magical metals, and the blend of iron and graphite and even titanium, a high-quality blade indeed.

Yet the musk of the man who wielded stopped here, before the bridge itself. His musk had much sweat in it, but no zing of other magic. The women's fruity scent also stopped between those posts.

The bitter smell of fear too.

The smell of rotting fish, from across the canyon, yes, it was faint, but it was clearly here. The broken grass, the tentacle trails, hobgobbles.

The scents of the man and women both head into the woods behind him. The women smell of utter terror, and of serpent too — of his quarry. The man of ... lust and porkish pride, of being the rescuer, not of being hunted, or the hunter.

Yet this bridge ... why it was drawing his attention despite his quarry going in the opposite direction ...

Jagger knew of the existence of mimics. Many had a flaw in their mimicry. Some did not.

The wind was far too hot now. With the graying skies it should of been cooler, not hotter, unless ...

Another dragotroll was being released.

The very thought chilled Jagger to the bone.

Just as a dozen hobgobbles slithered out of the wood across the canyon. The leader out in front, twice as big as the rest. In their arm tentacles, all carried several the dark wicked spears known as gulgen spears.

"Death wull not stop us!" the leader said, "The gurl is ours!"

Fools, but what a strange outcry.

Jagger drew his broadsword Chaserist.

"Then you must defeat me," Jagger said.

"My pleasure," the leader said, "Tendrins, Wind of Torment!"

Hobgobbles leaders called their minions tendrins, and all the hobgobbles behind the leader slithered to the edge of the canyon, so they all were his minions.

Each flung a spear at him.

Spears that started swirling.

Flying faster.

And faster.

Right at Jagger.

Guided by his calm heart, Jagger summoned his inner sunfire, like a sun within him, and with it, circled his blade.

"Pathetic," he said, "Whirlwind Shield."

All the spears crashed into the whirlwind. Exploded. Their shards blow back. Slashing the hobgobbles.

They all stood firm. None were killed.

Somehow.

"Pathetic Whirlwind," the leader said, "Gud name. Such a pathetic shield. Tendrins, Rain of Pain!"

The wounds of the leader ... started healing? Strange. Hobgobbles shouldn't regenerate. The lesser hobgobbles all retained their wounds and they bleed dark blue blood.

The smell ... of the most rotten fish ... from the leader?

The lesser hobgobbles each flung one their spears up high and, turning in a steep arch.

They'd land on him. By him.

Time to turn this around.

"Fools," he said, "Time to go."

And he leapt back.

Triple Whirlwind Shield flung him back far and quick.

Right into a mossy tree.

Just as the spears pin cushioned the place he had been standing. And all around.

Missing him by fraction of an inch.

He rolled along the tree. To its side. Waved good-bye.

The leader roared. "Follow him!"

Good.

The leader charged onto the bridge.

Followed by his smaller minions. Only one at a time fit. Yet the planks themselves smiled?

Ah.

Just as the leader and as many followers as could fit the bridge filled it the planks split open and swallowed them all whole.

The shocked hobgobbles waiting their turn got gobbled next.

Then the rope bridge settled back to its deceptive self.

CHAPTER 26
ROMEO

Romeo ... shocked ... his turn ...

The cheering whispers of the bearded oaks ... Juliet and her fruity smell overwhelming the musty forest ... his own cheeks hotter than the roasting rocks ...

No even the crows cawed?

Wow.

Good timing, but ...

Juliet ... her full six feet of sexy in heart-themed blue bikini-wear right before him and ... her strawberry pink heaven on earth ... not a dream.

Wait ... maybe ...

"Juliet, you don't have to—" he said but she nudged his mouth shut.

Clearly as gentle as her talons let her, at least.

"Sssshhh, silly," Juliet said, "It's not … well known but … unless you … with me … in this form … as our first … well … then … undress me."

The silence was so potent. More potent than … than … brainfart. Damn …

"I …" Romeo said … and …

He always dreamed of it yet never thought …

"Let's … you know," she said, "I don't want to wait. Really. Please. I don't know when we'll have this kind of chance again and … I'll *feel* … more like … you're my lifemate … if we do … you know … *now*."

Romeo blinked. "Did you just say … what I thought …"

She giggled.

Nodded.

Nervous, but not unhappy.

"Yup," she said, "Let's … fuck. Please? It's a … clawgirl thing. Trust me."

"I do," he said and slipped off his vest, then stopped.

"Wait," he said, "Do you want to undress me?"

She held up her talons and grimaced like a sad puppy.

"With these?" she said, "I'll need you to do *all* the undressing. *Enjoy.* I **so** totally know you dreamed of … undressing me and … sorry it won't be in my human form but … please?"

He nodded. "Dream come true."

Juliet giggled. "Exactly."

And he slipped out of his slacks.

His boots.

Good thing it was warm out.

No, not warm. Hot. As hot as Juliet. If beauty could burn, she'd inflict third degree burns.

No.

Fourth degree.

And the shade wasn't that cool, and the planty whispers might as well be cheers, and the rock beneath his now bare feet roasted them even more.

"Oh," she said, "I can do the heels, but the rest …"

Leaning back against the bearded oak, Juliet did some kind of slippy kick and got her heels off, clonk clonk.

They even landed right next to his boots.

Wow, was she graceful, despite those talons for feet, clicking and gripping the rock below them, as graceful as a gorgeous sexy songbird. Her feet were so much like her talon hands, except bigger, stronger.

Her heels weren't even in the slightest damaged.

"Nice kick," Romeo said, "How do I take your top off? As much as I dreamed about it …"

She giggled. Turned around.

A breeze of fresh strawberries and cream, delighted his nose and loins, especially with that classic hint of cherries and vanilla.

And wow, brushing her silky golden hair away, her shoulder blades, *so* exposed. There was only a blue strip with three pink hearts along a vertical line and …

"See those pink hearts?" she said, "They're actually buttons."

"Ooo," he said and did what he dreamed so long.

Unbutton those three pink hearts. Top. to. bottom. Unwrap her heart bra top. She even turned around as he and—

She hugged his face into her chest.

Soft **strawberry** *bliss*. So **warm**. *Soft*.

"Enjoy 🤍" she said and kissed the top of his head.

Better than any dream. Like a real-life wet dream come true. Her sigh, her resting her chin on his head, so sexy sweet.

Romeo slipped his hands onto her soft warm sides.

Ah. And down them.

Over her hips. Lush lush hip. He he sooo longed to rub. To hold. How many years had he seen them strut so loin-achingly sexy and now ... dream come true, dream to rub and rub and rub and so silky sleek like the best kind of pudding but for the hands.

How many nights he could not not fall asleep, simply yearning for this faceful of strawberry boob bliss and lush hips under his hands.

He kissed the spot between her breasts.

Heart thunk thunk thunk.

Licked her.

!

She tasted as sweet as she smelled. Of sweet strawberries and cream, but not too sweet, and with that hint of cherries and vanilla ...

He licked her again.

She giggled. "You want to eat me all up?"

"Do I ..." he said and slipped his fingers into the once forbidden bliss underneath her miniskirt.

To the once forbidden panties ... wait ... underneath the top strap of her miniskirt ... soft silky scales all around ... and so round up front and ... unbuttoned the one big pink heart button to girlie good heaven.

He finally, after years of dreaming of it, dreaming of aching for a stray lucky glimpse underneath, actually slipped her miniskirt off and ...

Romeo gasped. "No panties?"

Juliet chuckled sultry. "Nope. This miniskirt ... too revealing for them."

And — oh heaven ... strawberry heaven ... she pressed her whole warm soft body against his.

Turning him gently. Oh so gently in her arms. In her breasts. He grabbed her ass. Her fine fine ass. Such soft heaven.

And followed so so willingly.

Her blissful beloved minion.

More devoted than any mere hobgobble.

He let her press him against the tree. Its soft soft moss, but nothing compared to her breasts, her fine fine ass. The moss was moist, was so cool, yet refreshing. A nice contrast to her warm silky body pressing him into it.

If only this bliss would last forever.

They slid down. And down. And down.

His ass to mossy curved root. A chair of sorts. A very nature low chair.

Her ass now over his lap. Her hips holding him so sweet and he entered her and ... oh oh oh she moaned and ... oh oh oh his faceful of her chest and oh oh oh ...

And aaaaah. Like a keg of ale ... bursting open.
Eventually empty.
And so so satisfied.
They held each other. So warm. So gentle.
Till ...

CHAPTER 27
ROMEO

In the peaceful silence, Romeo listened to his own heart thumping, of Juliet's quiet pants, of the trees didn't even need to cheer them on anymore.

Romeo savored Juliet and her soft strawberry heaven. Holding her, her pressing him gently against the mossy tree ... she was softer, warmer than any moss, yet something was on the tip of his tongue ... but what?

"Hey, Romeo," Juliet said, "My thighs. You haven't ..."

"Good point," he said and rubbed her thighs and wow, so lush, so soft ...

He gave them a squeeze.

She giggled. "You *so* **reeeeally** wanted me."

"Still do," he said and hugged her even snuggier around her slim waist.

He could stay here, like this, for ... way way waaay too long.

Her pleased sigh, she definitely knew it too.

"After we marry," she said, "I'll ... you know. In my human form. Lots and *lots* of sexy time. And ... I'll wear my sexiest outfits when I can. Like this one. You *sooo* like them."

He gave her such a snug hug ... this strawberry soft bliss of her boobs ... idea ... actually ... never would of thought ... never would of bothered but ...

"You ..." he said, "It is true, as a clawgirl, you really love coin?"

"Yessss, but ..." she said.

"You handle our coin then," he said, "Forget Honey Heart Resort tonight. Let's head back to town. There's a competition. Combat competition tomorrow. With a *very* nice prize. Very, *very* good coin. I'll win it for you."

"Oh Romeo ..." she said, "You ... I ... I think ... I love you. I know ... nononono, we mated in my clawgirl form. That must be it. It's my first so ... you know."

"We've been friends for a while," he said, "Now we're more."

She sighed. "Lovers ... love each other."

"And you never expected a human to love you in this form," he said.

"Yessss," she said, "You don't know ... how scary it is. Those dime dreadfuls ... like ... I should be awesomely evil like them but ... I don't want to be like them but ..."

"You are awesome," he said and gave her another snug hug.

"Really?" she said, "How so? I ..."

"When that prince dumped you," he said "You worked so

hard to prove him wrong, but lucky for us he did. Imagine how'd he react if he ever discovered you're a clawgirl.

"Ooo, yeah," she said, "I kinda … hoped for the best. Like maybe … a royal renouncement of the bounties on clawgirls or something but … no, you're right. He'd never … I would sooo get killed, and horribly too."

She hugged him even tighter, but not painfully so.

"You sure you want to marry me?" she said, "I … I know what patrons often say. About us honey hearts. Why marry the mess when they could get the good stuff for some coin and avoid the rest? So … I understand if you … you change your mind. It's not like … well … I am a mess. And we haven't exactly dated and … the way I treated you well … not exactly the nicest … and … well … you know."

"I want the rest," he said, "Sure, you haven't been the nicest, but … you know that garden in front of your room, I know you're the one tending it. The other girls leave theirs all to me."

Even Vivian.

At first he thought she loved tending it but after their sword fights started … but that blue-haired girl Melissa loved to go mediate among her daylilies, even while he tended the garden, and their chit chat here and there, wow, was that sad expression for real.

But Claudia insisted on Romeo getting *every* **single** *detail* perfectly right and correct. Petals plucked. Dirt dug right. Weeds removed by the roots.

At least Fleur was never to be seen. Much. Except, sometimes, overseeing him silently from her window.

"Well I ..." Juliet said and pressed herself against him so sultry he couldn't help but sigh in pleasure, especially with the soft moss cushioning him, giving him a sweet soft and refreshing contrast.

"I do ..." she said, "I do *want* to marry you. Now. A life with you, you wanted adventure, right? I ... me too. Staying at the resort, now, no. Just no."

"Me too," Romeo said, "Let's find our own future together."

"Yessss," Juliet said, "No one's going to accept me like you have. Not in this form. I think, I have some ideas, for adventures, but first win that competition. We need funds. Bad. My own coin won't last as long as you think. Not once we're on the road."

"I know," he said, "Aunt Tilda made a point not to let me hold onto too much coin for that exact reason. We'll have to be careful about what we tell Aunt Tilda."

"I have ... some ideas there," she said, "Marrying with me means I'm free of debt too and ... the journey to the university I'd want to get into ... the way to get in even ... she knows it'll be dangerous."

"And no doubt will want me to protect you," he said, "But without putting me in too much danger ... or else ..."

"I know," she said, "And my clawgirl ... background ... I might ... no, I *know* there's a dragotroll out there, somewhere, and ... not just a dragotroll, but if we're alone, maybe, well, I ... I could try to learn to defend myself better. In my human form. If you ... would teach me."

"Definitely," he said, "But ... it won't be pleasant. I'll have to be tough on you or else ..."

"I know," she said, "You handled me being tough on you, I can handle you being tough on me. I can't go clawgirl often or else ... you know. I don't want us to end up on the run. That's why ... sexy serpent time ... now rather than ... you know."

Wow was Juliet nervous.

Romeo gave her another reassuring hug.

"I do," he said, "You know why?"

"Why?' she said.

"Because snagging a clawgirl wife," he said, "The best kind of wife I could hope for. Especially you."

Gently, she pulled away from him.

"Sit on your knees," she said, "Trust me."

He did.

And she rolled back. Tugging him with her. On top of her — umphf.

Stopped halfway?

"The jumping raptor?' he said, into her breasts, again.

Such bliss.

Yet how he was on top of her, yet still had a faceful of her strawberry bliss chest and —

"Fuck me again," she said, "On my prey. My next meal. Let me savor my mate desecrating this bird bitch's body before I eat her raw and all clawgirlie."

Her voice had a sinister hangry side to it yet ... he loved how she trusted him to her this side of her.

Romeo entered Juliet again. Pumping and pumping like this dream would end the moment he didn't pump enough.

Her panting ... oh oh oh he was panting ... oh oh oh they were panting ... panting like puppies in heat ... fucking like dogs in heat ... and dogs were so awesome ... this was so ... oh oh oh oh —aaaaah.

Romeo pulled up and looked deep into Juliet's big blue serpent eyes, and kissed her as big and deep.

"I'm yours to enjoy," she said and grinned so sultry beaming back that ...

"And I'm yours," he said.

And this time, she kissed him back long and deep.

Just as a boom rang out nearby.

CHAPTER 28
KRAK RIGUT

Krak Rigut once again tasted the muddy soil beneath his tentacles once more. Tasted the foul forest air that reeked far worse than any dried seaweed bed. The filthy birds and gamey rodents nearby were more disgusting than any rotting fish.

Up above, filling the craggy thick branches, those filthy crows cawing noisy all because they were once again denied their filthy fresh corpses.

So far.

The heat of the place wasn't bad. Not good. But not bad. Worthy of Krak conquering it for the Baelzog to burn down. Fertilize into a proper swamp land for hobgobble kind.

Even that lowly bridge mimic was not enough to truly end Krak once and for all.

Death shall never stop him.

Never again. Shall death stop a true hobgobble.

A gift from his beloved Krotha Rigut. That death shall never separate them again.

That death shall soon never separate any hobgobbles from their kind again.

But the tendrins who died with him, their power, their experience, as small as it was, when it was cruelly cut off by that bridge mimic, all of it fused with him, made their leader even stronger, in raw power, and experience.

They will be avenged. Their kindred soon shall have never-ending life like Krak. Soon.

For inside himself he could feel true power surging. Squeezing into a core. A true demonic core.

One that would grant him even greater power.

A power great enough to strength his beloved's own core.

And both their cores, together, and their clan shall all revive. Be granted never-ending life like Krak and his beloved Krotha.

It was power so great … it already made clawgirls serve Krotha!

And soon, him as well.

That pathetic clawgirl chosen for reason no hobgobble could comprehend, that bitch would soon serve him, devoted heart and soul, whether she wanted to or—

"Beloved," Krotha said, "It is time."

And she slipped so quietly and lovely from out of the shadows under the putrid green bracken.

Stayed far smaller than her true wonderful size. Small enough to ride on the head of a red fox infected with her strongest spore. With empty eye sockets were the spores entered its brain, the beast now oozed a delightful bright green from all orifices, an ooze that evaporated into a lovely fishy smell only his beloved smelled of best.

"Another human warrior," Krak said, "has come. With a potent blade. Not as potent as the boy's, but worthy of your magic."

"Excellent," Krotha said, and the fox she rode on trotted closer, "You are strong enough now. I pass the bond of my clawgurls to you. Use them well. Their training as whores shall prove useful later, if their warrior skills ... hold up."

Using clawgirls as whores for spying and assassinations ... normally the training took far more resources, but that a human resort should train so many of them so readily and unknowingly ...

Both of them chuckled.

The bond, ah, Krak could feel it like five more tentacles that stretched and, pathetic, those icy things called emotions, fear and worse, self-pity and filthy bitches.

"I shall use them well," Krak said.

"The ritual," Krotha said, "to claim the chosen clawgirl as ours is complete. Go and train her properly."

"As you wish, my beloved." Krak said, "She will weep for her failure to come to us willingly. I will track her down and ... beloved?"

Her joyful shutter ...

"My three-eyed crows," Krotha said, "have already found the one we seek. She mates with the boy right now. Hoping that boy will save her from her rightful duties. She must help be his death. Kill both humans for me, and bring me their blades. Their blades should be enough to unleash the final seal."

Krak couldn't help but grin at the implication.

"The other seals have been undone already?" he said.

"Of course," Krotha said, "Sacrificing two of the clawgirls who refused their duties, despite my attempted to train them properly, pity, but they proved far more useful in death."

"Any more clawgirls to be found in these parts," Krak said, "Without warrior training these may die too quickly, and reviving them is far too much for you, my beloved, and far too much of an honor than they deserve."

"More than a few more," Krotha said, "Once the last seal on Lord Foulest is released ... the resort shall be our next conquest, my love."

They both chuckled again. Their clan shall be avenged.

Their young shall be revived.

And humanity will meet their doom.

But first: the boy.

CHAPTER 29
JULIET

Juliet, argh, she, like a tentacle was wrapping around her brain. Inside her head. Slimy and and and

Around her heart.

Inside her chest.

Somehow.

She ... she was already on her knees. Th hard, hard stone ground. Curling up, oh oh oh. The cold hard ground against her scaly legs ... nonono, not so bad ... really ... ugh.

Romeo even was already in his slacks again.

But she was nude against the dead and half-eaten jumping raptor ...

Its gamey flesh still fresh and tingling the back of her throat. So savory and just moments ago, so, so made her so feel *alive*.

But now ...

Nonononono.

She was bare in the scale and and and—

She wanted more. More blood. More flesh.

Gulp.

She tore into the jumping raptor. Eating even more.

Beyond what her stomach even wanted.

But ... she couldn't ... help it. Her body ... no ... something ... insisted on it.

On stuffing herself, and ... her body obeyed.

She obeyed.

Yes. Obey.

She was a clawgirl after all. It was her duty to obey. Right?

Boss Tilda even insisted she obey. Human or clawgirl, obeying was what ... you know.

And her claws were so so sharp. Eager to rip into the bird. Tear into more of its flesh. Break its bone. Drink its marrow.

So good.

Real food.

Not like that *human* food.

Because humans were ...

Juliet gasped. "No ..."

But her body trembled.

Her claws all too ready for the next meal. A meal her body was already insisting on.

"Romeo ..." she said, "Run. From me. Now. Before I ..."

But she was already lunging.

At him.

CHAPTER 30
ROMEO

Romeo was so shocked, time stopped.

The bearded oaks stopped their whispers.

The thunder booming in the distance vanished.

Halted.

The murk beyond the clearing froze. Froze more solid than that barrel of ale left in the cellar over winter.

And Juliet going vicious pink clawgirl on him ...

Her bright blue eyes as terrified as they were crazed ...

His back was already against the mossy tree. Pressed against it as hard as he could. His harpe by his pants. By his feet.

And too far to reach quickly enough.

No.

Reach by hand.

How many dime dreadfuls had heroes use their feet to wield their weapons ... not many.

Time to outdo some dime dreadful heroes.

He grabbed the hilt with his toes.

While her ruby red claws stretched out — for his throat.

Flying slow.

But steadily closer.

And closer.

Pink lightning crackling between her talons. Ruby flames flickering around the bolts. Smelling of burn air and ... roasted cherries?

Weird.

But no weirder than yanking his harpe out with his foot.

Slow.

Too slow!

He reached for her wrists.

But not enough time!

(Unless ...)

He slipped down the mossy tree and — ack!

Too slippery!

Just as he hoped! The sudden jerk downward jerked his limbs up just as fast.

Fast enough for his hands to catch her wrists.

Yank them away from his throat.

Above his shoulders.

Just as the dull outer edge of his harpe slammed against her gut.

Weakened her impact.

Slammed time back to normal.

Just as the moss by his ears exploded.

BOOOOM!

Roasted moss and cherries. Ick. Auntie Tilda's favorite local salad. Just toss in the strawberries and cream sauce, but Juliet's scent now, Romeo couldn't help but smirk.

And enjoy.

Her painful gasp. Her wonderful strawberries and cream breath.

He smirked even wider, but kindly.

"Change of mind?" Romeo said, "Or first marital spat?"

Her fanged snarl. Her pain wasn't just physical.

"I mussst ... obey," she said, "I ... I ..."

"Obey who?" he said.

"*Him*," she said, "Massster Rigut. He comes and and and — I *mussst* **obey**!"

BOOOM!

Lightning and flame. Right by his ears.

But he refused to flinch.

"Since I appreciate the warning ..." Romeo said, "I'll trust that—"

And he slammed the pommel of his harpe into her scaly gut.

Her painful gasp. Jerk. She wasn't accustomed to fighting. The pressure on him eased a touch.

Another slam eased it further.

"Change back to your human form," Romeo said, and slammed the holt into her gut again.

Enough to make her legs crouch and tremble.

"I ... can't," she said, "You ... please don't ssslay me, but ... I ... umphf!"

Nailed her in the gut again.

Dropping her this time.

"Sorry about this," he said, "But ..."

He swung around her. Yanking her wrists around her back. With his knee to the nap of her beautiful back, he pinned her to the ground.

Grabbed his vest. Tied her wrists together with it.

Her hisses and whimpers ... whoever this Rigut was, whatever that Rigut was, he'd pay dearly for slaving Juliet.

Romeo grabbed his harpe with his hand and — ah!

The smell of rotting fish!

Hobgobbles to his sides!

One side — CLANK!

Then the next — CLANK!

His harpe clanked their spears away. Sliced away their tentacles. Cut them down.

But more and more came.

Just as Juliet tried to kick him with her taloned feet.

Talons crackling with pink linking and ruby flame.

Romeo flipped around. Sat on her ass.

His feet pinning hers.

While fending off more hobgobbles.

Cutting them down.

And their corpses ... turned to ash that swirled away?

When a chuckle erupted above him.

An all-too-familiar, watery chuckle. From the first hobgobble to ever speak to him.

And to dead by his own hand.

"Awaken yur true power," it said, "Chusen One."

Romeo looked up and ...

"Didn't I kill you?!" he said.

"Death is no barrier!" it said, "Fur I am Lord Rigut!"

CHAPTER 31
JULIET

Impossible.

Juliet knew it was impossible.

A hobgobble controlling a clawgirl?

Impossible!

Yet the mossy soil fouling her mouth, her body shoved against the mossy ground, her gut aching terribly so, and deservingly so for attacking Romeo who thank the—thankfully he didn't die, and didn't kill her either.

But there was no mistaking that stink of rotting fish.

Deep down her whole body screamed in glee, like she won a bag of gold, over her master being so close and attentive.

Damn hobgobbles. That she ... she would be *his* slave.

Her body ... she whimpered, hissed ... thankfully Romeo only tied her up with his vest. Pinned her down—as painful as it was—getting skewered would be worse.

So much worse.

And using his harpe with his feet. Wow. That ... if only he didn't have to use it against her but ... least he used the dull edge.

Not ... all guys would of used the dull edge.

Especially after ... sleeping together. So many, only a fuck and then forget the girl, but ...

Romeo really meant what he said. She really chose her. Wanted to be with her.

And and and ... since she was the Chosen one ... she ... she chose Romeo!

She ... really did want to be with him. Her body shuttered.

And agreed?

Yesss!

(But for how long ...)

CHAPTER 32
JAGGER

Deep in the bracken smelling of rotting fish, crouching and hidden behind the mossy oaks smelling of rodents and serpent, the smell of fresh air from a clearing not far away.

Jagger heard what he needed to hear.

Time to do what he must.

Wait.

Above him. Around him. Faint, but ... sniiiifffff. Yes.

The smell of serpent girl. No.

Sniiifffff.

Many serpent girls.

The breeze. Hot. Slow. But ... from the trunks? Ripped moss?

Ah!

Clawgirl archers in the trees!

Jagger whipped out Chaserist.

Circled over him. Sunfire Shield.

Just as a rain of arrows poured down at him.

Ripping through the bracken.

Burning it. Shocking it. The smells, that zing of magic.

Their claw powers. Into their arrows.

Causing all the arrows to explode upon contact.

The clawgirls were in their typical scandalous leotards, sandal thigh boots, and fingerless elbow gloves. Hoods and mouth cloth hiding their identity.

Almost hiding their scents too.

Almost.

But not enough against his Bloodhound Nose.

Like predatory grasshoppers they were. Flipping over to different branches so evilly graceful and dangerous. No doubt bonded to evil masters. No doubt they needed to die for it.

They loosed more magic-enhanced arrows at him.

His Sunfire Shield protected him.

So far. But he couldn't remain this defensive for long.

Not taking even a single warrior to back him up, a mistake, but he was far from a weakling.

Back against a tree. His whipped Chaserist up.

Flinging a slash up into its branches.

Destroying them.

Boom of splinters ripped through tree and clawgirl alike.

But no cries?

But no arrows yet either.

Jagger dashed around the tree and—ack!

Dark serpent eyes greeted his own.

Paralyzing him to the spot.

Pain ripped through his gut. He fell to his knees.

"My firsssst man flesh meal," the clawgirl said, "so wonderful!"

Jagger was still paralyzed. His mission a failure. In more ways than one then.

He couldn't even respond properly. Not yet. His last form. Releasing now. No other—

Suddenly pain stabbed all over his back.

And he could only gasp. His strength leaving him.

As the clawgirl licked her chops.

And bit into his neck.

CHAPTER 33
ROMEO

The rotting fish stink only piled on the horror of the reality of the hobgobbles gathering around Romeo.

It ruined the familiar smell of the bearded oaks, of the dead and shredded jumping raptors, and him sitting on her ass, him being too aware of pinning Juliet and her soft yet scaly body underneath him ...

That she wasn't struggling nearly as much anymore.

But the largest hobgobble right beyond the clearing ... Lord Rigut ... back from the dead ... and far more powerful.

Just like some dime dreadful.

It was Romeo's time to shine but ...

He couldn't dash across the clearing. Now while pinning Juliet down. He dared not risk flinging his harpe. Or anything too dramatic. Now while more hobgobbles edged closer and closer around him.

"Romeo," Juliet said, "I ... I'm in control of myself again."

But that fanged grin of the largest hobgobble Rigut ...

"I'm not sure it's you're doing," Romeo said, "That Rigut bastard's smiling too creepy."

"Let me go!" Juliet said, "You ... you can fight all of usss at onsse—if you need to, yessss? You're a sword massster, and I ... I'm too inexperienced to put up a real fight."

"True but ..." Romeo said.

"But nothing!" Juliet said, "Off! *Now!*"

"Okay okay," Romeo said, and got off her.

Helped her up.

Just as more hobgobbles struck with spears.

Him—bang!

Deflecting them.

His arm aching.

But not enough to stop him.

From slicing a few more down.

Or Juliet from clawing a few bloody black and squealing death cries from the ground.

But more charged in.

Juliet screamed.

In terror.

Romeo cried, "Back-to-back!"

And back-to-back, they went. Facing off against the hobgobbles.

Together.

Her pants, terrified but ... exhilarating.

Fighting not just to save her, but with a real live clawgirl, as more than a lover, but as his wife!

Boots firmly on the ground, Romeo readied to defend her.

Her scaly warm skin again him, despite making love twice already, his heart raced with cold sweet sugar, but this ...

This was better than any lemonade.

The hobgobbles now edged back. Even now, it was clear they hesitated to do in a clawgirl.

"You've got to tell me what's between you clawgirls and hobgobbles," Romeo said.

"Not the time and plassse, idiot," Juliet said, "Focus on them."

"And not your fine ass against mine?" Romeo said.

Juliet huffed. "Exactly. I'll fuck you again later."

And the click of her flicking her claw open and hazardous.

"Okay okay," Romeo said, "I'll focus, wify"

Juliet sighed. Clearly annoyed, yet ...

"Good," she said, "I've read those dime dreadfuls too. And there has to be some necromancer raising that Rigut again and again."

Romeo wasn't the only ones nervous at the click of her claws.

Their rotting fish stink ruined her strawberry sweet smell anyway.

But not for long.

"Good plan," Romeo said, "I'll clear this horde, and —"

"I'll kill that necromancer," Juliet said, crouching more.

Till she gasped.

"Wait ..." she said, "Where did that Rigut go?"

"Oh. *fuck,*" Romeo said, looking up and ...

CHAPTER 34
ROMEO

Romeo looked up up and up. In the bearded oak.

On a branch as craggy as Aunt Tilda's flaring nose.

Hidden by the rotting stink of the hobgobble horde.

Of so many bloody hobgobble corpses.

Of a sky grayer than dull steel.

And the not-so-distant thunder right that moment.

No time.

Rigut. That huge undead hobgobble.

Two spears.

Lunging down at Romeo and Juliet.

Using their back-to-back position against them.

But after everything Romeo trained for.

After years of turning his chores into training.

After Aunt Tilda took care of him. Despite him reminding her of her lost sister so much.

After waiting so long for Juliet to acknowledge him.

To want him as much as he wanted her.

No.

It wouldn't end here.

With everything he had. Years and years of frustration turned to joy and hope. Romeo shoved Juliet out of the way.

Well beyond of Rigut's downward slashes.

Almost getting skewered himself.

Almost.

Boom!

Rigut's spears exploded the ground.

Flung Romeo back.

Right into Juliet.

Them both into a wall of hobgobbles.

Through them.

Juliet screamed. "Romeoooo!"

But she was hugged him. And he heard the ground being torn underneath them.

Underneath Juliet.

Until bang!

They slammed into a bearded oak.

CHAPTER 35
CLAUDIA

Claudia was trembling, *trembling* and from the chilling thrill of her first true battle. Not just the chill of the icicle sliver deadly snug and still within her bosom.

Ready to stake her dead if she dared to defy Master Rigut.

How she even managed to climb these thick craggy trees. With their trunks of slippery moss. Even in her reptilian form …

Like her sister, no, *sisters*.

And then leapt around the branches so gracefully and easily like a dance she'd do for a patron yet … no.

Not she stood up high in these trees, it wasn't just poor stammering Fleur, it was all of them. They had to back each other up like they did against the human warrior they just felled. Prevented him from doing anything except using some shield magic.

Just like they did when trying to climb up these trees.

Each again in their own tree. Even Vanessa.

Now their scimitar bows were strung and arrows ready to down death down again.

But they first had to find that boy Romeo.

At least Fleur in the next tree over still had her hood and mouth cloth up. Her sunny long hair hidden. Just like Claudia with her long red hair had been doing.

BOOOOMMMM!

From nearby?

And so loud it rumbled everything.

Enough to make her sandaled boots slip a touch on this thick craggy branch.

But no. That chill in her bosom.

Claudia steadied herself.

It is time. Clawgurls. Be my tendrins and kill the boy!

Claudia nodded. Her body already moving, and not by her own will.

Just like before.

CHAPTER 36
ROMEO

In the strawberry warm silence of Juliet holding him from behind, Romeo, for a strange moment, was utterly amazed at the size of the clearing. At the lopsided gray circle at least a dozen paces wide. The bearded oak right in the middle.

And at the claw marks *deep* in the rock leading right to them.

The smell of broken burned stone. A smell so strong he could taste it.

"Juliet," Romeo said, "You—"

Juliet whimpered. "No. My scales. They must be marred. And I just molted!"

Romeo gave her arms a compassionate hug. That he still even had his harpe ...

"I'll kill them all for you," he said.

Juliet gulped loud and nervous.

"Okay, yeah ..." she said, "You keep Rigut and his hobgobbles here, while I hunt down necromancer."

"You can track him?" he said.

"I'm a clawgirl," Juliet said, "Of course I can. What did you think I did before I came to the resort?"

"Good point," Romeo said, and stroked her scaly sweet hands.

"Points, I mean," he said.

Juliet tsked, but not unhappily.

"And I love you too, hubby," Juliet said, "Now go!"

And Romeo charged at the hobgobble horde.

Ripping out a roar of bloodthirsty joy at them.

CHAPTER 37
JULIET

Bare in the scale, with the wind whipping her long blonde hair all around, even in her face—especially in her face—Juliet dashed as fast as her taloned feet could carry her, but nonono, she *just* knew it wasn't enough.

Not yet.

Yet the cool musty wind against her bare scales ... that need, that desire slow down sluggishly rather than shiver cutesy for some lusty patron, and after all that crazy hot yet oh-so-cozy heat ... sigh.

She actually missed it.

As embarasssssing as it was to be nude in the woods.

With the taste of raw, gamey jumping raptor still in her throat no lessss!

But long ago, in her wormling days, she went bare in the scale so often that—nonono.

Focusss.

Those mossssy trees littered the ground with countless leaves, and she didn't hesitate to run over them now. Tear and poke with her foot talons. Leave as much of a trail as she could for Romeo to follow.

She breath deep into her mouth. Let the air flow over her tongue. A long flowing breath expanding her chest and that she was now bare in the scale, she didn't even need the support there that she did in her more human form.

Strange how she got so used to support there.

Enough that she bared her fangs in a wide freeing grin at the thought she'd no longer have to worry about some annoyingly flimsy top stretched to the tight breaking.

Least for now.

She'd definitely wear it for Romeo. Once she finished off this necromancer—ack!

Talons seized her throat.

Choked her! From behind!

Stupid stupid stupid!

"S-s-sorry, Juliet."

Juliet rasped. "Fleur?!"

Then to her side: "Like, not just Fleur, silly."

"Vivian?!" Juliet said.

More talons grabbed her own. Yanked them behind her back.

Hard.

Juliet was on her knees before she knew it.

And from the ferns ... a hobgobble riding a poor fox that ...

oh. my no ... spore slaved fox. Slaved even worse than Fleur and Vivian.

And Juliet knew, deep down, she was next.

CHAPTER 38
ROMEO

Romeo tasted the thrill of battle, the thumping music of his heart, the thumping of his boots to hard gray stone, the swoosh of hot breeze here and there, but ...

This battle still tasted too much like rotting fish. Time to make it more like sliced calamari.

Well done.

Just like he dreamed of endless times, the horde of hobgobbles was upon him.

And he was slicing them down.

Scores of them.

Yet the numbers of hobgobbles kept increasing. A horde was a horde after all. He was no hero unless he took them all down.

Drove the fear of humanity's toughest into them.

Proved humanity was no prey for these monsters. Their masters.

That Juliet and other clawgirls like her deserved to live among humans as wives and sisters, not enemies. Whether they were bitchy snobs like Fleur or carefree goofballs like Vivian.

(Not that Fleur or Vivian were clawgirls, but ...)

Against these numbers Romeo needed another technique. Using his racing heart as battle music. The taste of rotten fish and sliced calamari shoved him forward. Readying a technique, he only heard of.

In dime dreadfuls.

Prove he was a sword master. Despite what Aunt Tilda thought.

Only one chance.

Spears swung at him from all direction. Rotten blue tentacles whipped around. Reaching for him.

Perfect.

The gray stone. Hot. Hard. And solid beneath his feet.

Feet that danced. To his heart's thump. And right into a spinning slash. The Spinning Slash Bash!

Quick.

Deadly.

And thrown.

Ripping through all the hobgobbles around him.

Ripping them all apart.

Their spears apart.

Leaving only their bodies ... wait. No bodies? What the ... wait.

Oh no—the next trap.

CHAPTER 39
ROMEO

The thrown slash banged loud and clear into the bearded oak in the center of the clearing. Only paces away? Woh. Romeo had fought well into the clearing.

The stink of rotting fish and vaporized calamari a nice reminder of his sword mastery.

Except in the trees around the clearing, oh no, above their mossy beards and in the craggy winding branches.

Gorgeous clawgirls in typical bright leotards. At least … three of them.

Forming a ring around him.

In thigh sandal boots over legs he wouldn't mind wrestling with. Fingerless elbow gloves sleek with armor that could deflect lesser blades. Their cowls of their hoods covered busty chests while hiding their hair, and sinister mouth clothes hid all but their big beautiful but wary eyes.

Worst of all, their bows. Each was a pair of bone scimitars joined by the handle. Drawn with a wicked arrow.

An arrow flickering with each their own clawgirl power.

Ahead of him a fire clawgirl in a ruby outfit and even more toxic bright green glare.

To his left a water clawgirl in a bright blue outfit and brighter blue eyes that were … deeply sad, but determined.

To his right a brown-garbed clawgirl with an arrow with violet haze by its blade? Her hood hid even darker eyes.

"Romeo," the fire clawgirl said, "Your turn to die now."

That voice … the same that was very, very picky about him tending her garden. The same that nagged him over every single repair. The same that grumbled whenever he finished the remaining strawberries instead of her.

"Claudia?!" Romeo said.

"What of it?" Claudia said, "Master Rigut says you must die, and we exist to serve him now."

Like Juliet almost did …

How did Juliet escape his control?

"Where is Master Rigut?" Romeo said, "That coward already ran?"

A snort from the dark-garbed clawgirl on the right. That familiar scornful sound from under the dark hood …

"Vanessa?" Romeo said.

"Manflesh is sooooo good," Vanessa said, "We all just had some very good—but you, young and even tasssstier. Master Rigut is the besssst thing to happen to usss."

Vanessa already killed someone? And enjoyed it?

Okay, she has to die. Before she gets better at it.

A sad sigh from the blue-garbed clawgirl on the left.

"Sorry, Romeo," she said, and sighed so sad again?

"Melissa," Romeo said, "Don't give up. You too Claudia. I'll find a way to—"

Claudia loosed a fiery arrow at him.

Zipped so fast.

But predictable. Bang! Deflected by his harpe. The dull outer edge.

But, oh no, Claudia already had another arrow ready?

"Nothing can sssave us," Claudia said, "or you."

CHAPTER 40
ROMEO

Romeo grimaced.

Since when did Claudia get so good at archery?

Or did clawgirls really have innate archer skills like the dime dreadfuls said?

Or was this that Rigut bastard's doing?

Romeo could even taste a hint of cherry-touched serpent in the smokey flames of the deflected arrow now smothering arrow only paces away on the gray stone. No doubt Claudia had that cherry scent, given her lush ruby hair, even if it was right now hidden by her ruby hood and cowl.

He eyeballed the distance between him and the bearded oak in the center of the clearing. The closest cover.

Several good sprints away.

No sign of that massive hobgobble that called himself Rigut.

Yet.

Claudia was right in front of him. Had higher ground in the tree at the end of the clearing. No chance he could out run her arrows running toward her.

Toward them.

No sign of that necromancer Juliet went after either. The murky woods didn't reveal a hint of what happened. Neither woodland critters squawking away or dashing away.

Or monsters more suited to Shadow Forest.

But if there were more than just hobgobbles around … could Juliet fend off other clawgirls? Especially if she didn't know about them?

The bearded oaks surrounding the clearing provided plenty of branches for the three clawgirls to leap around him. Dodge his thrown slashes easily.

No doubt the blue-garbed Melissa, still to the left, could. Her depressed mediations at the resort suggested … a more athletic past. Vanessa in the dark garb to the right … he didn't know much about her. At the resort she avoided him like he was a troll that would infect her with awful ugly whatever, and she admitted it to his face, except whenever Aunt Tilda was around.

But her dark hood … dime dreadfuls had warnings about some clawgirls and those that hid their eyes …

And a dash to the bearded oak in the center … no.

Too obvious.

Except … what else should Romeo do?

Wait.

There was some sunlight reaching through the thunderclouds above. Enough to give him a shadow ahead of himself.

Put the sunlight against those clawgirls view of him. Except they were looking down and the sun, even if it peeked through the clouds, was above them, and ... wait.

Vanessa. Where was she?!

"Enough play time," Claudia said, and loosed another fiery arrow right at his chest.

No.

Three?!

Spreading out! To his everywhere on his chest. Burn him to death quick and horrible.

Just as Melissa loosed a trio of watery arrows at him.

At his head. Heart. And waist.

Speeding too quick to dodge. Leap back.

Or roll forward.

Only one choice now.

His heart thump thump thumped. Battle music once again. His feet ready. Already stepping. Turning.

Spinning Slash Bash!

Throwing the slash quick and fierce around him.

Boom!

The fiery arrows exploded. The watery arrows too.

Leaving behind clouds of smoke and steam. Both so hot they scolded his mouth and nose. Tasted of cherry and blueberry and serpent?

No. Clawgirl.

This was his chance.

Romeo dashed through the scolding smoke. His cover.

And reached the bearded oak in the center.

Just as Vanessa slipped out from behind the oak.

"Boy flesh!" Vanessa said.

Her hood was off. Dark eyes serpent—from the corner of his sight.

"Your turn to die!" Vanessa said.

Her grin as fanged as any dime dreadful clawgirl.

But Romeo was leered down at that, woh, half exposed chest of groin-hardening pleasure. Not as big as Juliet's but tanned a sexy toasted color and—

HISSSSSS!

"Look at me!" Vanessa said, "Not my chessst!"

Romeo grimaced. "Not the blade I want to put in you but …"

He did. Thrusting the whole crescent blade of his harpe through the side of her gut.

Vanessa gasped, squirmed. "No. I can't die here!"

"Too bad," Romeo said, "A death for a death."

Whoever she killed needed avenging. To prevent more deaths by her.

Her dark leotard gave little resistance. Not against the potent power of his razor-sharp blade. Her skin scales some more resistance. But a pang later. Nope.

Nowhere near enough.

His harpe sliced up through her. Her insides. Up through her heart.

And the curved tip jutted out from her breasts.

Breaking … CRACK! A silver of ice with it?

The utter shock in her face …

"I'm … sorry," Vanessa said, "I … I only did what I thought I had to. Please—cough, cough—don't kill me."

She coughed up blood. Clutched her chest.

"My heart," she said, "It's ..."

"Gone," Romeo said, "You're done for, Vanessa. Like any clawgirl deserves that goes killer bitch for fun and flesh."

"I ..." Vanessa said, "I'll will take you with me!"

She transformed. Her skin going dark scaled. her hands into reptilian talons.

Talons that slashed at him.

But he jumped back.

Kicking her off his blade — and it sharp inner edge ripped out of her.

Her shock. Gasp of more blood.

And she toppled over.

"VANESSA!" Claudia said, "You ... you ... DIE ROMEO DIE!"

CHAPTER 41
ROMEO

Shocked Romeo couldn't even gasp. Claudia was behind him? How?!

His pa would be so disappointed. Losing sight of an enemy like that.

But that shadow. Long and growing. A gorgeous girl with twin scimitars. Fiery scimitars. Smelling of burning cherry. Lunging at him from behind. From the fading smoke of the cloud the destruction of her arrows before made.

Now only paces away.

No hesitation now.

Like pa drilled into Romeo, charges were all about timing. So his thumping heart. Battle music he turned swiftly to.

Lunging back.

Ruined Claudia's timing. her fiery scimitars roared as much as she did. Her fury insane.

Was she really that close to Vanessa? Wasn't she Fleur's sister? Not Vanessa's.

But no matter. They were enemies right now.

Her or him.

So he swept himself between her blades.

Her sneering gasp. Only powered his pommel right into her gut.

Full strength.

Her oomph. Stopped her lunge instantly. The full impact shuttering through her slim but beautiful body. That leotard clearly reducing the worst of it.

But it gave Romeo the moment he needed. To knee her again in the gut. Hard. Her leotard banging his knee back harder. Her skin scales deflecting the worse of it. Banging his knee back even worse.

But years of fix-it work, years of sword training, his knee was no weakling.

It pounded a solid gasp from her. She was clearly now low of breath.

But clawgirls were serpents. They could go a while without air. Without passing out.

So her weak snarl. "Melissa! Now!"

"Goodbye, Romeo," Melissa said, "A death for a death."

From above him?!

CHAPTER 42
ROMEO

Romeo didn't hesitate this time. His thumping heart was already musical. Ready to end this craziness. The rumble of thunder so close by only emphasized the danger coming closer and closer the longer he took.

No hesitation anymore.

Melissa made her choice. Like Vanessa did.

Time to pay for it.

Romeo threw a slash upward.

Right at the branch Melissa was on.

Right as Claudia lunged again. Hugging Romeo tight.

Python serpent tight. His breath leaving him.

Ruining his aim.

BOOOMMM!

Melissa screamed.

Thump!

Collapsed onto the ground. A dozen paces away.

Moaned.

And passed out.

But Claudia didn't let go. As warm and sultry as her horrible hug was …

Claudia growled.

"You ssspared Juliet," Claudia said, "but usss, no. Why?! Why is she so ssspecial?!"

"Melissa …" Romeo said, "isn't dead."

"She would be," Claudia said, "if I didn't—"

Romeo hugged Claudia back. Tender but secure.

"I know," Romeo said, "You think that. But Juliet fought. Rigut off. I know you. can too. For Fleur's sake. You—"

"Don't speak of Fleur!" Claudia said, "I'll kill you. For her sake. For our sake. I want to live. Even if it's as some evil clawgirl. I don't … want to die."

"Me neither," Romeo said, "Let me—"

"No!" Claudia said, "Master Rigut. He'll … he'll kill usss both. All of usss. You die and we live. You live and we die. Badly. Painfully. *Please.* Don't hate ussss."

"I don't," Romeo said, "Not even Vanessa. I just …"

"Just didn't know what elsssse to do," Claudia said, "Just like me. I mussst kill you. So sssssshhhh. It'll be over sssssoon."

"Really," Romeo said, "Then …"

"Then what?" Claudia said.

"Time to have some fun," Romeo said, and grabbed Claudia's fine, fine ass, and woh, was it a pair of awesomely soft cheeks and that leotard didn't exactly provide the best coverage so …

Claudia screeched. Jolted.

"*You* **pervert!**" she said.

And loosed her grip. By *a* **lot.**

Enough. To *shove* himself free of her.

Stumble back. See how she was unarmed now. Her scimitars on the ground. By where his feet used to be.

Claudia gasped. "No ..."

That sad, sad look. Worthy of Melissa.

"My time now," Claudia said, "Make it quick. Please."

"My pleasure," Romeo said, and sliced vertical, through her bosom, and CLANK!

Another ice sliver destroyed?

"Free now?" Romeo said.

Claudia yanked her moth cloth off. Even grimaced. Clutching her chest. As is he cut her, rather than just the sliver and leotard.

"You sweet idiot," Claudia said, "but no. Master Rigut's bond is like ... how usss clawgirls controlled hobgobbles. But reversed. There's nothing but—"

Fleur screamed. Echoed from everywhere.

"CLAUDIA!!!!!" Fleur shouted, "Romeo ... *DIE!*"

CHAPTER 43
KRAK RIGUT

Krak blended perfectly into this filthy stinking lone tree. Right at the top. Among its hard twisted and scrawny branches. Too much like a starved dead tendrin.

Except tendrins couldn't change color as well as Krak Rigut.

Blend into their surroundings nearly as well.

His hefty spear, he almost threw it. Almost used to destroy both that human boy and the rebellious clawgirl while she hugged him tight below, but Krak didn't expect such ... rude behavior from the boy or such a pathetically foolish reaction form the clawgirl.

Honestly, she should of celebrated the boy's stupidity. Given the boy pleasure to die of.

Not screamed and jerked back.

He'd need to train them as whores. Proper whores. Force

them to fuck human men of all sorts till their own bodies meant nothing to them — except as weapons.

At least his other clawgirls had arrived.

And the new one. The one this boy prized most of all.

The one who would now be his death.

And her own breaking—their great lord's revival.

CHAPTER 44
ROMEO

Romeo didn't freeze. Not this time.

But he knew better than to argue with a distraught snob like Fleur. Knew he needed to listen carefully to the echo of her distraught scream.

Ignore the thunder nearby.

The smell of Claudia and her cherry clawgirl scent. Forget the warmth of groping her fine, fine ass. Ignore the biting must from the destroyed branch of this bearded oak in the center of the clearing.

The disappointment his pa would feel if he knew his son had been nearly ambushed again, and so soon.

No doubt Fleur wasn't alone.

The crackle of ice?

From above!

Yes. The bearded oak. It had countless branches.

In bright blue clawgirl garb. With cowled hood and

mouth cloth. Bu those big, cold intensely blue eyes ... no doubt it was Fleur.

With a bright blue scimitar bow. Aiming an arrow cackling of icy sparkles at him.

Right between his own eyes.

Fleur snarled. "G-get. *away.* f-f-from. my. *sister!*"

"Stuttering?" Romeo said, "Since when did you stutter?"

Claudia snickered. "Always. Except around patrons."

"Really?" Romeo said, "I ... never knew. Sorry."

"D-d-don't apologize," Fleur said, "You h-h-have to die. I-I-I have to kill you. K-k-kill you like you killed Vanessa. And Melissa."

"Melissa isn't dead," Romeo said, "Just unconscious."

Claudia huffed. The sound of scimitar against stone.

"Thanks for the save, sis," Claudia said, "I'd stab this assssshole in the back, but his sword skills ... Vivian!"

Fleur wasn't alone.

Not by any means.

Romeo was so ...

CHAPTER 45
ROMEO

No.

Romeo knew better than to ever give up. Giving up. Same as dying.

Especially here.

Now.

Worse. That would doom these clawgirls to a life of honey horroring rather than honey hearting.

But in the long shadow of the bearded oak. Among the crowded craggy branches twisted and stretched long and winding.

In the closest branch above him. Near a half a dozen paces above him.

No doubt but ...

A quiet sniff. The breeze. A chill now. Carrying the rumble of thunder nearby. Perfect for this moment.

Time to make pa proud.

Because that hint of a rosy scent …

Romeo couldn't help but smirk.

"Vivian," he said, and turned toward his lovely nemesis.

And there she was.

On the closest branch to him. Looking down condescending as any clawgirl enemy should.

She was in clawgirl archer garb as rosy pink as her long lush hair, except, woh, her leotard had plenty of suggestive white hearts over it too?

And exposed more than plenty of her upper bosom. Proving her chest was a peachy heaven as big and beautiful as Juliet's own. If she wasn't a good few inches shorter than Juliet the patrons might of selected Vivian as more beautiful than Juliet …

Her thigh boot sandals hugged long lush legs he wouldn't mind hugging himself.

But her slim hourglass to a guy's doom was cocked as cocky as her bright violet eyes grinning wicked happy.

Her slim arms spread wide. Their fingerless elbow gloves even had pale pink steel guards.

A pink scimitar in each hand.

And around her. Like a halo of thin spikes.

Rosy pink sabers. Floating in the air. Around her.

"Time for us to like," Vivian said, "Fight for realsie. No Boss Tilda holding me back anymore. I like, *so* totally want to kill you."

Romeo smiled back. "I so know. After I failed to save you …"

"**Exactly**," Vivian said, "and like totally cheating on me with Juliet. You owe me. *Big*."

"But your virginity auction …" Romeo said.

"The bastard who won," Vivian said, "was just some corpse puppet controlled by Master Hobgobble. I am sssooo still a virgin it hurts."

She even squeezed her legs together by her crotch. Wow.

"Girls," Vivian said, "get lustsmitten as much as you boys do. We just totally don't get to like act out on it as much. Not the way we want to."

"Don't worry," Romeo said, "I'll deflower you the right way."

"You better," Vivian said, "Try at least. I am ssssooo going to kill you now. So die by my hand. I *need* some excitement. For realise."

Romeo chuckled this time.

"With back up," he said, "or one-on-one."

"What do you think?" Vivian said, "Massster Rigut isn't much for dramatics. All of usss at once. But you better die by my hand. Or me by your hand. You better not hold back or I will ssssooo totally like kill you."

"I know," Romeo said, "Enough foreplay. Let's get—"

Flash!

BOOO

CHAPTER 46
ROMEO

OMMMM!!!

Thunder. Exploding nearby.

Too nearby.

The sound ripped through everything. Pounding Romeo. Shaking him. Jolting the ground. The bearded oak rattled. Cracked. It wasn't hit but a tree close by was. His hearing. A ring. A loud ring everywhere. His taste. Shocked metallic.

Romeo stumbled. Wobbled. But no.

Stand firm. Like pa trained him to.

This fight. The fight of a lifetime. First fight of a lifetime.

For soon — he'd have far more fights of a lifetime.

If he survived this one.

If.

The flash almost, almost made Romeo miss Vivian. Her attack.

But his heart thump thump thumped louder than any thunder. Positioned his feet for a counter before he knew it.

Because Vivian. Above him. Right above him.

Lunged down. Diving through the air. Cutting through it. Like a thrown dagger.

Already attacking.

Laughing her pink-obsessed ass off too.

Yet her laugh. So distant. So far away. Compared to the ring. The loud, loud ring. Metallic taste. No.

Blood?

And that halo of pink sabers around her.

All shot down at him.

Straight down.

Fast.

Faster than her.

Vivian was now behind it. Diving at its center.

At him.

But well behind.

So when the pink sabers struck. Same moment Romeo spun around.

Spinning Slash Bash.

Deflecting all the pink sabers. Like hail smacking a tiled roof.

But Romeo knew better than to relax. He parried up right away. As quick as he could. As quick as pa drilled into him.

Yet no. He was almost too slow.

Almost.

Again.

CLANK!

Vivian crashed down. Pink scimitars first. Right into his harpe. The dull but round outer edge.

Vivian laughed. "Nice parry."

Her scimitars slid off his harpe. Off each side.

"But not nice enough," Vivian said.

As she flipped around midair.

Slammed her feet right into the back of his head.

Stars. Metallic taste worse. Far worse. Stumbling.

And Fleur? Snarling?

A few paces away. Standing there.

Blue scimitar bow drawn. Icy sparkles cackling wicked around its blade.

Romeo couldn't help himself.

"Why do you hate me?" he said, "I ... I don't understand."

Fleur gasped. Shocked like he struck her hard — yet he didn't.

"I ... s-s-sorry," Fleur said, "I ... don'thateyou. I ... I ..."

Stuttering again? And was that ... her big blue eyes were so wide and terrified like ... like ... it couldn't be. If only she didn't have that mouth cloth on.

Thunk. Behind him. Vivian landed several paces behind him.

Thump thump thump went his heart.

"Sorry about this," Romeo said.

With the thump of his heart. Enough that he flung a slash at Fleur. Quick but easily dodged.

(Hopefully.)

Her gasp. Shit. She wasn't dodging it? She was rooted to the spot.

And loosed the arrow.

No the arrow split into a ring of arrows. A storm of icy darts.

One that exploded his slash. Left an icy fog. Hiding Fleur from him.

"*Nice* one, Fleur," Romeo said anyway, and flung a slash behind him.

At Vivian dashing toward him.

Who flipped over it.

Shot her pink sabers his way.

When Claudia growled above well him? Ack! Her shadow. Yeah. Aiming arrows down at him.

"Don't compliment her, you perv," she said.

Thump thump thump went his heart.

His feet moved before he could think. Just like pa trained him. Just like his overseen matches with Vivian.

Spinning Slash Bash. Deflected the pink blades. The fiery arrows boomed into smoke above him. Iced arrows exploded into freezing fog beside him.

And a boom? Crackle crackle. His other side? While his untamed hair was pulled by some unseen force? Made even more wild?

No.

He knew of this from dime dreadfuls. Read about it plenty.

Lightning clawgirl power.

Another clawgirl under that hobgobble's control!

CHAPTER 47
ROMEO

Just the smell of the lightning. A familiar strawberry scent. With that lovely hint of cherry that he got to savor every Tuesday.

Better than any leftover fruits too.

"Juliet?!" Romeo said, before he looked. Saw when he knew he'd see. Sent his thumping heart racing too fast to move with.

Between the last of the bearded oaks and him. Right over those deep tracks left by her talons before they last saw each other. After she saved him from that hobgobble's massive attack.

Juliet was there. Back and oh no.

For standing tall and sultry was Juliet in a lightning blue leotard with pink lightning bolts patterned over it suggestively. Amazingly great suggestion for her doom to mankind kind of curves.

Those thigh boot sandals too. Legs he wants to feel up again. Especially now. Even her fingerless elbow gloves and their pale blue steel guards looked supersexy on her.

That she had lightning blue scimitars with pink handles. That they were joined together by the pommels to form a wicked bow. A bow drawn with another arrow crackling with bright blue and pink lightning.

But her eyes ... as lighting blue as her power and terrified.

"The necromancer got me," Juliet said, "Ssssorry. I ... I have to die now, don't I? You or me, and ... sssorry. I exist to serve—"

Juliet loosed her arrow.

Claudia was in front of him. Fleur was to his other side. Opposite of Juliet.

All of them loosing their arrows at him.

And Vivian ... the shadows behind Claudia. Vivian was above him. On the branch again.

Spearing her pink sabers down at him again.

Spinning Slash Bash was his only hope.

But he slipped.

Crashed to the ground.

The arrows all missing him. Screams from Juliet and Fleur. Of terror.

Boom by Fleur.

Crackle by Juliet.

Claudia screamed "Fleur!"

Romeo gasped. But no. They weren't hurt. Neither of them.

Their leotards were ... protective? Really?

Really! Yes. The dime dreadfuls talked about that all the time. Sexy yet deadly. The fabric could not only deflect the danger many ordinary weapons posed, but it upped their skin's protective nature several times so that only seriously magical blades had any hope of cutting them.

His harpe ... must be really special then. Pa ... what was pa? Really?

Both clawgirls were cringing. Too shocked they were fine to react right. Attack him. Even Claudia was too frantic about Fleur to end Romeo.

But not Vivian.

CHAPTER 48
KRAK RIGUT

Krak knew it. Hiding up here. High on top of this stinking tree. This was it. Shadow the pink-haired clawgirl's attack.

Be the true final strike.

He'd destroy the boy. Claim the blade his beloved needed. And it would only cost him another clawgirl.

Pity.

She could fight well. Better than the others.

But her death was worth it.

That blade ... his beloved would love it. Love it as much as they loved each other. For it was the last key to freeing their true masters. A baelzog hidden deep within the mountains here. The smell of ash and flame so ... so familiar. So faint yet so close.

And the Rigut Clan would be the ones to revive them. Bring humanity's doom.

And it would all start with this boy.

CHAPTER 49
ROMEO

In that instant. Right above Romeo. Up in the bearded oak. On the closest branch since it lost its other nearest.

Against the rolling dark clouds.

The booms and rumbles so close by.

The metallic taste in his mouth ... gulp.

Vivian stood sultry cocky. Her hood and mouth cloth down. Her grin wicked sinister. Her rosy pink hair so long and lush and very clawgirl of her.

The moment Vivian said, "Gotcha goofball!"

She dived straight down at Romeo.

And Romeo knew he couldn't leap up in time.

The aches over his whole body. It refused to move yet. Refused to move fast enough., The shock of his bad landing too powerful. Too shocking.

He couldn't dodge her coming attack.

But he could see up her boob crack in that leotard. And woh. As amazing as he ever imagined it. Boob heaven it was.

But ... was that a silver of ice?

By her heart?!

No.

Damn hobgobble bastard ...

Vivian dove so quick. Yet so slow. Romeo couldn't react. Not in time. Not anymore.

Not with any normal movement.

At least he could hear his heart thumping again.

Thump thump thump it went.

And ... last chance.

Last move.

A move specially for a girl he loved to tease. To mess with. Mess with as much as she messed with him. As much as Aunt Tilda would allow it. A barrier they both tried to shove aside.

With the thump of his heart. The music of battle. And a last gasp.

Romeo cried out. "Puributcher!"

And with all his strength flung his new technique at her. A flying slash it looked like. A big massive one.

Her gasp.

Grin.

"That's totally it!" Vivian said, "Bring it on!"

Her pink sabers whipped out of the rock around him. Formed a shield in front of her.

A shield that did nothing, of course.

To her utter obvious shock. Violet eyes so wide, so big Romeo couldn't help but laugh.

"Enjoy a Technique," he said, "That's worse than death!"

"And worse than totally obvious!" Vivian said, and she parried with her pink scimitars.

But they missed it too.

His Puributcher—not slowed in the slightest.

Or deflected.

Not even when it slashed apart her whole outfit.

The sight of sexy heaven. Curves he only could dream of before. Only in his wettest dreams he dared. Curves he yearned to do more than watch and slap, miss with his harpe. Curves he's seen jiggle and flow sexy since forever at the resort. Curves that sent his heart racing stupid happy.

Even for that instant. It was enough.

She screamed utterly, utterly horrified.

Jerked to cover herself. Flinging her scimitars away. Fouling up her attack.

Even—smack!—her landing. Beside him. That gust of rosy scented air. Her musk. his cheeks went blazing. His heart racing.

Her moan.

Whimper.

"You ... win," she said.

Crying? No ... cheeks not so blazing now. Heart icing over.

"Did I ..." Romeo said, "go too far?"

Vivian was curled up. Nude. Yet utterly utterly gorgeous. A peaches and cream desert for the eyes and loins.

Yet ... she was so ashamed. Terrified.

"Don't ... like apologize," she said, "You totally—WATCH OUT!"

Before he knew it Vivian rolled onto him. Grabbing him. Pressing her whole body against her. Her boob heaven chest against his bare chest. Her bare stomach against his. Her wet dream legs against his slacks.

When he saw it.

That huge hobgobble, Rigut. Spear headed down. Along with the hobgobble. Right at them both. That powerful attack. The one that threw both him and Juliet nearly out of the clearing.

And this time. No dodging the full impact.

"Death shall not stop me!" Rigut said, but his tentacles ...

They were turning gray?

So was his head.

Romeo. With the last of his strength. With everything he had. His heart thump thump thumping faster and faster and this had to be timed perfect!

With his harpe. Its crescent blade.

"I love you Vivian," he said, and hooked the spear—right above her heart.

Sent a flying slash to power their roll away.

Just as BANG! The spear plunged—not into them.

But into empty gray stone.

An instant later Rigut joined the stone as rubble. Big chunks of the tentacled freak lay in a pile. Broken from the impact. Sliced by the harpe. His fishy stink even worse now.

But no guts anywhere.

"Death cannot claim ..." Rigut said, "Impossible. The bond ... where ... oh beloved, curse that human—"

Boom! A fiery arrow shattered Rigut. His stone remains. Now just pebbles and dust.

Claudia huffed, but fell to her knees? Hard.

"Curse yourself," she said, "For slaving us. And your own weakness."

Fleur fell to her knees too. Hard.

"The b-b-bond," she said, "It's ... gone, and ..."

Her wet cough ... the bond wasn't gone in a good way.

CHAPTER 50
JULIET

Juliet couldn't help but gasp.

It wasn't just the chill of the icy fog around her, frosting her leotard, soaking her whole body like some ice bath horror, all from those ice arrows from Fleur, arrows that Juliet's own leotard somehow protected her from.

She couldn't help but tremble, and not just from the freezing cold. All she had wanted to do here was discreetly shed her skin. Not run into another mimic. Not get into some crazy fight. No.

But honestly, she read enough dime dreadfuls that she should of known that her getup would protect her from the elements. She had to read those ridiculous books. No real choice not to. Not if she wanted to stay a top choice at the resort. So many patrons read those books that they always appreciated a girl who knew them well, and a honey heart ...

But well, she knew her clawgirl archer getup, as skimpy as it was, could protect her from regular weapons by upping her skin scales' natural protectiveness, besides the garb's unusually protective nature, but even magical weapons? This skimpy stupid thing? Really?

It really did.

Enough to freeze her stupid again. Freeze so still it was beyond what humans could pull off and she never, since she got mistaken for a human girl, she never risked freezing such steady. So still.

Ever.

How could she become so sloppy? All from ... this?

The fishy stink from that last hobgobble was terrible, but fading away *finally*. But her bad memories wouldn't. Not for a while.

That she was so willing to kill Romeo.

That he was so willing to let her die.

Romeo, by accident, almost ... almost killed her. Like she said he should, and well ... how could she claim to love him back when ... when ... the rumble of the thunderstorm ... it shook her as much as her own stupid thoughts shook herself.

The sharp stink of must. From the blasted oak tree. All the damage to it. In the middle of nowhere forest too.

At least she gave him her virginity. That should count for something. Right? But ... she struggled to stay standing. She ...

Juliet fell to her knees. Hard. Banging against the stone ground. It hurt but she deserved it. How could she not? She didn't hesitate to go killer clawgirl on him when he needed her most.

It wasn't her that saved him from that awful hobgobble.

It was Vivian.

Despite certain, horrifying death had that awful Rigut survived.

A death, the very thought of it, made Juliet tremble. Even now. Tremble as much as the rumbles of thunder nearby. Nearby but fading away. The chill, the icy fog at least made her skin feel clean...ish again. Like it could wash away the awful feeling of what she had become.

Almost become.

Juliet hugged herself. Not that she deserved it. Even deserved to be saved like this. No wonder she felt so cold. She was too cold to deserve Romeo. No wonder he went over to Vivian so quick. Their love was so fake. So easily forgotten. It only happened by luck. They were only friends after all.

Friends that ... not that she even treated him that well. Not like Vivian. Who gave him plenty of sexy during their crazy bouts. Even with Boss Tilda there to stop it. To punish her if she went too far.

Yet the pull within Juliet. Within her chest?

Wait a moment. Why ... wha ... why was there a pull within her chest. A tugging that shouldn't be there?

She was dying, of course, that must be it. Once the bond was severed like that ... just like when hobgobbled died after their commanding clawgirls was killed.

Now it was her turn.

CHAPTER 51
ROMEO

Back to the hard stone ground, Romeo finally realized that in his arms, the arms that held Vivian, were arms holding a legendary monster as well, doing something the legends said was never to be believed.

Trembling terrified.

Trembled like a terrified damsel in true distress. He knew for sure Vivian was not faking it like the legends insisted her kind were. Even if her archer garb was now quickly growing back, just as the dime dreadfuls claimed it would. A magical technique that would drain Vivian and shortened life even shorter.

But Romeo refused to let her go. Not now.

Not when she was a damsel he didn't know (yet) how to save.

Just like Claudia. Fleur.

Even Juliet.

He couldn't save them from the death that was certainly coming for them now. The dime dreadfuls always explained how bonded minions of the baelzog would die with their masters. Slow and cruelly, as punishment for their failure. Whether it was hobgobbles that failed to protect their claw-girl masters. Even clawgirls.

Especially clawgirls.

And no doubt that necromancer would of made the bond kill these clawgirls as awfully as it could all to punish them for their failure to protect their master.

A punishment Romeo needed to undo.

Somehow.

But how?

The rumbles of the rolling gray clouds were growing more distant now. At least the sun was breaking through more and more. Even if the shadows now were crazy long.

Almost as long as Vivian's lush pink hair.

The must of the bearded oaks was as sharp as his harpe. No. Even stronger now, and not just because Romeo had destroyed so much of the lone tree here.

The bodies of the jumping raptors would definitely attract worse creatures soon enough. The stink of rotting fish from the countless hobgobbles killed wouldn't deter nastier creatures of Shadow Forest from feasting on the corpses left here.

Even on Vanessa. She needed to die but ... sigh.

Why Vivian too?

Why Juliet?

Fleur. Claudia. Both still on their knees. But together now. After crawling to each other. Hugging each other.

Even Melissa. Still unconscious.

Romeo didn't know them as well as he thought, but he knew none of them deserved the kind of slow awful death that was coming for them. Pa would insist he end them with his own harpe. Grant them a less painful death. Mercy killings, yet his heart no longer thumped musical enough for him to bare holding his sword.

Let alone harm them even more.

The thunder rumbled so loud, yet so distant, like his hopes of true happy ending. The dime dreadfuls always had the clawgirls be femme fatales that needed killing. Celebrated their deaths. Wild and crazy sometimes, but always necessary.

Nothing like the real clawgirls here.

Except, maybe, Vanessa, who, no doubt, would not of gone killer clawgirl without that awful Rigut to push her in that direction.

Had he not stopped at that crazy bridge mimic. Had he simply kept walking. Kept to himself. Aimed to reach the resort in time. The supplies he was meant to bring.

But no.

Juliet would of certainly died. Not as awful a death, but an awful death. By mimic. A terrifying death. And no one would know. Ever find her remains. A terrible end.

Yet was this any better?

"Vivian, I ... I'm sorry," Romeo said, "How ... how do you ..."

"Sssshhhh," Vivian said, "Let me totally like enjoy your embrace till the end. I guess I totally need to die like the usual clawgirl villains, but ... I ..."

"No one wants to die," Romeo said, and hugged her firmly. Her lush body against him. Her trembling even more.

"But want and will," she said, "Totally different things. Was I like, a fun villain?"

She even looked deep into his eyes with her own bright violet ones. Not crying but frowning so sad. Her breath as rosy warm as she was. As the pink roses she so loved in the garden outside her room at the resort. The fragrant roses that were always cut for her room.

"The funnest," he said, and slipped his hand behind her head. Guided her closer. Closer.

And kissed.

A warm wet passionate kiss. Of longing denied so long their moans were as gentle and delicate as handling a husk of a beloved blade. Gentle as the breeze. The warm breeze blowing her beautifully pink hair into their faces. As gentle her brushing her fingertips against the side of his face. As gentle like all those near gropes he tried giving her during their fun bouts at the resort.

Gropes she always giggled about.

Only sometimes dodged.

And this kiss wouldn't end until Vivian did.

CHAPTER 52
JULIET

Juliet took a few deep breaths. Calm. down. now.

Gulp.

She could even taste the icy fog. The hint of Fleur in it. Of serpent too.

Fleur so needed to molt soon. Lucky her didn't do it *before* this battle that would of messed up her skin scales.

The must of the tree. Of the trees nearby. The rumbling of the thunderclouds didn't help. Not at all. They were worse than patrons grumbling about their incoming loss right before she threw the game their way without them realizing it.

Except for that prince that denounced her as too stupid for ...

Maybe she was stupid. Why else would she end up like this?

Yet ... Juliet could also feel ... it couldn't be, but despite

Juliet herself sitting on her knees, in this awfully skimpy archer garb she felt ... a second body? On the ground? Back to the ground. Hard hot ground. Covered with a ... a ... girl?!

Those movements, her own lips kissing yet not kissing and so, so passionate and yet so, so sad, and yet *no* ...

It couldn't be.

They were just like ... in front of her. Paces away. Vivian was on top of Romeo again, and whimpering something. Trembling and whimpering, and such an awfully long kiss. The kind lovers about to separate for far too long and maybe never see — wait a moment.

"Why can I feel ..." Juliet said to herself.

She gasped. Dime dreadfuls described this very thing when ... when ...

"We're bonded?!" she said.

CHAPTER 53
ROMEO

Romeo had to as shocked as Juliet at her words. Her cry.

Louder than the thunder ripping through the rolling clouds above them. Clouds flashing bright and furious. Growing a darker and darker gray.

The shock was enough to end his kiss with Vivian. End it loud and clear at the same moment Vivian did.

To gasp mutually too.

Romeo was as tense, as stiff, as hard as the rock underneath his back. Pa would laugh at his predicament now. Ma would too.

In fact, the musty air right now reminded Romeo of the attic pa had kept so many of his odd trinkets in. Treasure, he claimed, from his adventures with ma.

Adventures Romeo wanted to have with Vivian.

But unlike Aunt Tilda, his parents wouldn't of tried to

keep Romeo away from Vivian. Or Juliet. They would of encouraged this very ... well ... bonding with any, no, all of these clawgirls, yeah, they'd encourage him to ... well ... especially if they were bonded like Juliet just cried out ...

They be open to even more adventurous adventures. A pack of their own, so to speak, and he'd be their shared mate, kinda like a real clawgirl pack, but without the ugly abusive nightmarish side the dime dreadfuls loved to harp on about.

With Vivian still on top of him, Romeo, his heart pounded so fast and hard, her rosy warmth so pleasing that it was like he was in her rose garden at the resort again, but no. Romeo couldn't bring himself to try to sense if he could feel anyone else besides this dream come true girl on top of him. Her being as hot as the stone beneath him. Even in her clawgirl archer garb.

Especially in her archer clawgirl garb.

Gulp.

Her big violet eyes gazing down into his. Like big round flowers only from her.

"I'm ... your minion?" Vivian said, and gulp.

Far too loud and clear.

"I ... can you tell?" Romeo said, "I ... with you on me I ... well ..."

Vivian giggled. That perverted smile of hers ...

"I can like *totally* feel your feelings," she said, "Down there."

Oooh. His cheek became ... well ... almost as hot as the rock underneath him. Despite the dark gray sky. How it should be cooling things down now.

Or anytime now.

He even almost apologized.

Almost.

But a bit of courage went a long way, right?

"Anywhere else?" Romeo said, and gave her another warm passionate kiss.

A kiss she returned just as passionately.

Then sighed.

"Okay, okay," Vivian said, "I like totally know about this bond. Patrons like totally told me about it lots of times. It's in the dime dreadfuls, you know."

"The slave bond," he said, "Or the familiar bond?"

"So like eager to totally put your trouser blade in me," she said, "You can't tell the difference?"

"I ... good point," he said, "A familiar bond ... I should be able to sense you clearly. Sense you enjoying me, but ... if it's a slave bond, I should only be able to feel your presence, and ... well, besides your gorgeous body on me, warming me in ways I've only dared to dream of, sometimes, I ..."

Vivian giggled, smiling even more perverted this time.

"Looks like that new technique of yours," she said, "did more than just strip me naked."

And now, she wasn't the only one smiling perverted.

CHAPTER 54
KROTHA RIGOT

Krotha wailed.

Wailed as sharp and loud as the thunder booming around her. Lightning as black as the abyss her dead clan now lingered in, awaiting her arrival as well.

Lightning that was striking the gray stone everywhere, as she needed it too, charring the filthy green lichen everywhere black all around her.

She wailed again. As sharp and loud as her fox mount gnashing its fangs in well-deserved agony. Agony for failing her. Failing her love. Failing to move her fast enough to return to him in time to save him. Save her last true hope to reviving their clan. Restoring it to its prior glory.

But the bond with her beloved was cut. Gone. Vanished.

Severed worse than any tentacle ripped off. Worse than the new hole ripped gapping inside her. A hole filled with pure dark hatred as deep as ... a demon core. Her love's demon core!

But her love was gone. Death had claimed him too!

A death that must not be in vain. He must be avenged.

And Krotha knew exactly how. With his core soon to be inside her, her power would then be more enough to claim the lives of that boy and his delusional clawgirl traitors.

Remake them into proper corpse puppets.

For now there was only vengeance. Her true masters would inflict it well on the rest of humanity, but the boy and his clawgirls were hers, and hers alone to kill, destroy, torment to the ends of the abyss itself.

And those wretched clawgirls. How dare they fail her love! Let him die and dare not die with them?!

And Krotha could sense her spore cleared from one of them. Her magic too. That clawgirl's presence had faded, but not her life.

Not at all.

Yet.

That scolding tingle around every shard of the bond ... a purifying sword technique. That was it. One her love could never hope to stand against. Not without her close by to protect him. It was only a matter of time before the other living clawgirls were purified.

But the dying one ... and that human the clawgirls took down ...

So two corpses were near them. One near death, but recovering. Her spore was inside the wretched human that dared hunt her kind for so long. Twisting him as he lay unconscious. Turning him into a creature that could better serve her properly.

Help her end the human menace once and for all — once he awoke in a few days.

And that clawgirl whose body was ruined. Who was slain by that very boy that saved the others. Soon to be a corpse ...

And it was unlikely that boy would think to purify a corpse. An oversight that would soon cost him dearly.

More than dearly.

And that was just the beginning.

But first, some preparations ... some time ... a few days. That was all. And then vengeance would be hers.

CHAPTER 55
ROMEO

With Vivian side-hugging him snug and giggly happy, Romeo stood proud, his smile beaming brighter than the lightning in the distance. His harpe was more than ready to save his clawgirl girlfriends.

And girlfriends they would be.

Especially Vivian here.

Her rosy smell so delightful. Like side-hugging a garden rose.

But without the painful pricks.

But only paces away, Juliet was still on her knees, hugging herself nervous in that lightning blue archer leotard in thigh sandal boots and elbow gloves. The pink lightning bolts suggestive yet ...

The bearded oaks around the clearing were getting darker

and darker, but the sun wasn't setting yet. The clouds above were getting darker. The storm getting worse.

Yet no rain?

"Juliet," Romeo said, "You sure you don't want to get undressed first?"

"No, I ..." Juliet said, "I'm too weak, and ... you've already seen enough, right? No need to hide — to be modest, right? I ... you saw me bare in the scale. Now you get to see me, you know. Enjoy. I ..."

Okay. Romeo was sure now Juliet wasn't happy about his fondness for Vivian but he knew better than to argue now.

"Alright," Romeo said, "I will **so** enjoy this, Juliet."

Juliet smirked perverted?

"You better," she said and hugged her tummy, not her chest?

"Your pouch," Romeo said, "Put your coin aside so that—"

Juliet pouted so sour that Romeo almost gasped in shock. Almost.

"That nercomancer stole it," she said, "She took it all. Everything. And I ... I was forced to give it to her."

Juliet even shuttered. "Kill her and ... get my coin back. Please. I worked so hard for it and ..."

Vivian side-hugged Romeo even more tenderly.

"Me too," Vivian said, "That necromancer stole all our coin. Forced usss to give it all to her."

Claudia and Fleur, on their knees but holding each other tight and sisterly, both nodded too.

Romeo nodded. So clawgirls really did love their coin.

"I'll get your coin back," he said and returned Vivian's side-hug firmly.

"Everyone's coin back," he said, "but first, I'll free you all."

He listened for the music of her heart beat, and wow, was his heart thunking fast and furious, even if it was all because Vivian was side-hugging him all giggly and happy.

"Puributcher!" he said, and flung the massive flying slash at Juliet.

Juliet gasped. Tensed tight.

Shutting her eyes.

RIIIIIPPPPPP! Her outfit was shredded. Vanquished.

Juliet trembled, trembled so much Romeo couldn't savor the sight of her naked, as peaches and cream heavenly as the sight should of been.

"It's gone," she said, and gulped loud and clear, "I'm ..."

She perked up. "You're not enjoying this?"

"I don't enjoy terrifying you," he said, "As much as I do enjoy seeing your gorgeous body butt naked."

Juliet sighed, but not unhappy, giving that twisted smile reaching those bright blue eyes of hers.

"Then ... well ..." she said, "You wanna fuck? Again? I ..."

Vivian dashed over to Juliet? Pulled her up.

"We'll all like totally fuck him later," Vivian said, "but now we need to prepare for tonight. You know. Dinner. Then —first Romeo, you go save Claudia, Fleur, and Melissa. Then rest. Leave dinner to us. Your clawgirl pack. All those sword techniques, wowsie, you'll exhaust yourself and collapse before you realize it."

Romeo ... sigh, Vivian made complete sense, and them all fucking him later ... yay!

A dream truly come true.

And not the first today either.

CHAPTER 56
VANESSA

What about me? Vanessa wanted to say as she could feel her life still leaking out of her chest, slowly but steadily. Back to the hard cold ground. The air itself mustier than a graveyard and colder than the day ... the day ...

She didn't want to die yet but ...

The sky rumbled and bumbled high above her, but not even the sky would cry for her. She was so pathetic. Dying from her second hunt. A hunt that led to her friends being freed while she ... she ... why did she have to die?

Why do they get to live?

Everything was so, so cold. So, so slow. Even the flashes in the sky, the sky getting darker and darker. And so ... so ... slow.

The chirps and chitters of the woods so, so distant. The tree she had hidden behind as ruined as her. No.

Not as bad as her. It would live.

She would not.

It would loom over her grave. Mock her corpse. Feast on her body as it … it …

And the clawgirls she thought were her friends all giggled and cheered for their dear murderous bastard of a boy. The boy that killed her. That … that …

It wasn't fair!

True. Death shall not claim you—yet.

Vanessa managed to gasp? Who? No words came out yet her chest. It was pulling together. Knitting, closing and … her heart, it was beating again! She was healing!

A favor for a favor, yessss?

Yesssss. Whoever you are … she—

And this is what I wish you to do.

Wow. Vanessa giggled silently. This favor … a lot like a reward. She'd only need to take a couple of days to prepare.

And then, vengeance well-deserved.

CHAPTER 57
ROMEO

Now with all the surviving clawgirls free of that awful bond, and even with the familiar bond now fading, Romeo was once again sitting against the lone bearded oak in the center of the clearing, but this time, he was just watching the clawgirls work together to cook the dead jumping raptors into a proper dinner.

The meat even smelled like the best kind of blend of turkey and chicken roasted sweet, juicy, and delightful. The kind of meal ma would spend hours and hours preparing for All Winters Eve, and All Summers Eve too.

Parents that … maybe it was time for Romeo to go searching for them himself. With his own pack of clawgirls to back him up, clawgirls who were free, so maybe they wouldn't go with him. They might go their own way. Who knew? Free was free.

No need to dwell on it yet.

The rumbles of the thunderstorm were now coming from a distance. No rain. Not yet, at least, so lucky them. Any tracks from the necromancer wouldn't be lost.

Hopefully.

The smell of rain was faint. Beneath the deliciously roasting jumping raptor.

But it was there.

And as Uncle Jethro would say, trust your nose, and besides the lush beautiful smells of freed clawgirls, besides the must of the shattered oak branches, besides the faint smell of rotten fish fading even further ...

The smell of ash.

And worse.

Enough to ice over Romeo and his whole body. Today's battle was hard fought. Won for now. The necromancer got away, and none of them could return until they dealt with that necromancer.

Not one of them was save safe until they ended that necromancer and as soon as possible.

But tracking it, even on that supposed poor fox thing the hobgobble necromancer was riding on ...

The trees seemed to whisper comforting nothings. Celebrate a victory while you can, they seemed to whisper, and Romeo knew why.

It was only a matter of time before darkness fell in Shadow Forest. Before they'd all have to go high up in this lone bearded oak. Sleep in its branches to stay well out of the way of the creatures that would be attracted by this smell.

No telling what kind of monsters would come prowling

tonight. Whether they'd leave by daybreak. Sundown was coming sooner than any of them hoped, but they'd be ready.

They already faced worst.

And the scent of a pack of confident clawgirls should deter whatever came prowling for a while. At least during the last of the daylight.

And that should be enough. For now.

About the Author

Widely traveled, Jonathan Evan Hudson spends as much time studying life as he does writing gripping tales of fantastic adventures. From the giant redwoods of California to the deserts of Israel, his thrilling stories all draw on first-hand experiences and expand them with the fantastic and his acclaimed creativity.

Be the first to know!
For the updates and more:
www.JonathanEvanHudson.com

youtube.com/@jonathanevanhudson
tiktok.com/@jonathan.evan.hudson

A War Of Lust And Oak

Read Now!

The Elf Girl Effect

Read Now!

The acclaimed Jonathan Evan Hudson once again weaves an unforgettable tale brimming with spicy page-turning action and fast-burning enemies-to-lovers passion.

Meet the newly knighted Roo Vorshaya. Sworn to protect humanity in the isolated mountain town of Appleharth. Dreams of action-packed adventure and passionate love under a lovely but sinister strawberry-pink sky.

Love re-ignited by a whiff of the familiar peaches and cream scent of his long-lost childhood girlfriend: the notorious elven witch Amber Peaches.

And endangering everything Roo holds dear.

Love page-turner novels of epic fantasy? Love reading from dusk to dawn? Then go read *The Elf Girl Effect* now!

Martial Art Of The Phantom Saber

Read Now!

SUCCUBUS SLASH

The acclaimed Jonathan Evan Hudson weaves an unforgettable tale of thrilling action and adventure spiced with fast-burning romance and doused deep in epic fantasy.

Enter Miles Mayhem. Rich in friends and enemies. And a fat boy badass in the sword.

A seriously delicious smell of bacon and eggs smothered in spiced razor-hot cheddar signals celebration—and serious trouble ahead.

Trouble beyond anything Miles ever expected.

The perfect epic fantasy novel. A genre-enlarging feast for fans of sexy action and fabulous adventure. Read *Succubus Slash* now!

Sword Master Of Honey Heart Resort

Read Now!

Into Shadow Forest

Read Now!

A diamond in the rough the bestselling Jonathan Evan Hudson weaves a thrilling tale from explosive beginning to satisfying end in the awe-inspiring land of Grandcrest.

The talented twenty-something sword master Romeo Bladell yearns for love and adventure.

And at the musty edges of Shadow Forest. Near the towering high oaks bearded like stout old dwarves. By a canyon like a wound gnashed deep through in the granite. A canyon like the maw of a stone dragon.

A strange unexpected rope bridge hangs silently. Sinisterly.

Beckoning adventure—and danger unimaginable.

Enter *Into Shadow Forest* and savor the most spectacular of page-turning epic fantasy novels. Love unique monsters, riveting battles, and fantastic femme fatales? Then read *Into Shadow Forest* now!

Angels Of The Sword

Read Now!

Crossing Of Shadowed Death

Read Now!

The acclaimed master of fantasy Jonathan Evan Hudson once again shines through with his talented story-telling. Time to enter another stunning awe-inspiring world of dangerous demons, magical mayhem, and action-packed adventure.

A simple demon-hunting mission. The young and lonely Dirk yearns for amazing adventure, for gorgeously under-dressed dancer girls among the towering high ferns. Among the even taller pines of the hot and humid Fern Shadow Forest.

Pine needles everywhere. And so fragrant they made the finest of teas.

Sturdy reliable cobble roads of the Divine Empire cut through the whole entire forest. Providing the only safe passage.

Or so Dirk thought ...

Enjoy this sexy, action-packed epic fantasy adventure from the talented Jonathan Evan Hudson. Love to read an enthralling epic fantasy novel full of stunning rip-roaring battles with creative new monsters? Then go read *Crossing of Shadowed Death* now!

A TASTE OF THROUGH SHADOW FOREST

Once again the acclaimed bestselling author Jonathan Evan Hudson delivers an irresistible blend of passion and page-turning action in the fantastic land of Grandcrest.

At long last the one-of-a-kind sword master Romeo Bladell found the adventure and love he always yearned for. Sleeping high up in a bearded oak tree within Shadow Forest. Savoring the rosy fragrance of one of his new loves. Despite the grunts and growls of hungry beasts far below.

Until a terrible threat by a hideous monster threatens all he holds dear.

Enter **Through Shadow Forest** and embrace the most enthralling of page-turning epic fantasy novels. Perfect for fans of unique monsters, riveting battles, and femme fatales. Read **Through Shadow Forest** now!

CHAPTER 1
ROMEO

Romeo knew, he was sure that, crows should only have two eyes, but blink blink blink.

Yes.

It wasn't just eye crust getting in the way.

At the very end of a twisting thick branch of this oak tree, that big fat crow, it definitely had three big beady eyes.

Not two.

A third eye was right in the middle of its forehead. An eye that blinked back at him like the rest of its eyes. It stared intensely at him, like he was an earthworm that bird was eager to snap right up ...

The glare from the pale white moonlight, no mistaking it. The big fat moon cast a bright milky gleam over everything. As if Romeo had spilled milk everywhere again but without Aunt Tilda to yell and wallop him for wasting so much of the precious drink.

As if twenty something was too young to drink proper liquor, so he better still stick with ordinary milk, least according to Aunt Tilda, and since it was her home, so her rules.

But the way the fat crow was perched so tense yet cozy. It was alert, yet still faking some kind of relaxed search, as if it was searching for a stray corpse to feast on. How it bent the end of the thinning end of the thick branch with all its pump weight ... how the bend was nearly a pace down.

Far more than Romeo thought it should, blink blink blink. He was blinking but ...

Maybe he was just seeing things. He did just wake up from a strange dream he couldn't remember. His eyes were still crustier than one of Aunt Tilda's countless peach pies baked to steaming perfection.

But there was no chance of falling back to sleep now. Not with the crickets wailing like a little chorus of banshees everywhere. The frogs didn't help either. They were screeching their own frantic tunes.

Never mind the grunts and growls of giant beasts below every so often. The hefty huffs and sniff upward. The sounds came from at least halfway to this very branch.

And this branch was at least a dozen paces from the ground.

That hard stone ground.

Occasionally something big and fierce ripped at the moss closer to the bottom of the tree's thick trunk. As if pa were training his blade on the mossy beard of this oak. Or his dwarven grandpa and his beloved doubled edged axe.

But neither his pa or grandpa would attack the deep crack at the bottom. Shaking the whole tree a touch like the massive creatures below were doing occasionally.

Despite how thick and sturdy the tree was.

Then again, no one ever thought sleeping in Shadow Forest was a good idea. It just happened to be the only decent option for now.

Sort of.

He simply enjoyed the naturally rosy fragrance of Vivian as she slept soft and cozy, her back against his chest. Her sultry body sent his heart thumping louder than any cricket screech. Faster than any frantic frog cry. She was using him like the back of a loveseat, and honestly, he couldn't be happier for it.

Even here. As dangerous as Shadow Forest was at night.

And another reason that crow at the end of their branch ... Romeo better be extra cautious. It might not just be him it was eying for a snack.

No. Not just might.

Vivian was, as the dime dreadfuls would say, curved slim in the right spots, curved ultra-fat in the chest spots. Her long rosy pink hair softened her back pressing against him. His leather vest was wide open as he hugged her slim waist, her slim stomach snuggly. His crotch against her fine, fine ass, even with his trousers on, as Vivian had insisted.

Her breathing, slow and sleepy steady, unlike his racing happy heart.

Her grip, hugging his arms around her snug and tight.

But she wasn't defenseless.

Far from it.

Her leotard of pink with suggestive white hearts, along with her thigh boot sandals and fingerless elbow gloves and their guards all protected her, and magically too. From ordinary weapons and even some defense against magical weapons.

All because she was a clawgirl. A monster of legend so to speak, even if she was in her human form right now. She hadn't yet showed him her reptilian form. Not yet.

But he knew her skin could become scaly like a serpent and even more protective than her human skin, which, technically, was actually very, very fine scales that only looked and felt like human skin. Her hands and feet could go taloned like a reptile too and she could wield special powers with them.

But she hadn't yet revealed her clawgirl form to him—yet.

She must not want him to think less of her. As if he would. They spared forever at Honey Heart Resort, a resort they both worked at. Putting on a show for patrons, but of course, Romeo was always required to lose. Vivian always required to win—until some handsome rich patrons tried his luck and defeated her while she always went down as sexy and sultry as she could.

And wow, could Vivian go sexy sultry.

But just yesterday, she had been slaved into fighting as a proper clawgirl was meant to, against humanity, and they had fought for real.

Until he freed her with a ... perverted kind of purifying attack.

Thankfully her archer garb somehow recovered after a while as well, or else she so could have clonked him good, as he would have deserved.

Yet ... Romeo knew monsters of legend were real now, and yes, he had heard of three-eyed crows somewhere before ... but where ... where had he heard of three-eyed crows before ...

Good thing Vivian had her pair of pink scimitars. They were hanging sheathed off her thick belt. They could easily be snapped together by the pommels to form a bow that could fire magical steel bolts as long as her stamina lasted.

And did Vivian had some good stamina.

Romeo wasn't unarmed either. His harpe was a powerful magical crescent blade with a razor-sharp inside. Able to slice through the hind and armor of monsters of all sorts.

Even the protective scales of a clawgirl.

If need be.

But hopefully ... never again. His sword techniques were even better. They could fling slashes with unusual powers as well. Including the technique that saved Vivian from the life of being a slaved minion doing clawgirl evil.

Vivian murmured awake. "Romeo?"

"Vivian," he said and gave her a reassuring hug.

A hug she returned. Returned far too nervously.

"I just totally had a nightmare," she said, "Of the life I like, would have had to live, if ... you know."

Romeo hugged her snug again. "I know, and—"

The crow cawed loud and clear. All three eyes stared **hard** at Romeo.

Freezing him? His body ... it wouldn't move. Refused to move. Breathe even.

His sword ... he needed to reach his sword ...

But how?

"Romeo?' Vivian said, "Wha ... no, that crow!"

The crow cackled?! Romeo tried to grit his teeth, but no.

No movement.

Yet.

"Return to me, Vivian," the crow said, "and all will be forgiven."

Vivian gasped. Tightened her grip on Romeo.

"What?!" she said, "Never! I hate you! I—"

"What you think," the crow said, "doesn't matter. You, you and your kind exist to serve the Baelzog. Nothing more. Nothing less."

Romeo tried to snarl. But again. Nothing.

But Vivian hissed. Louder and angry serpent style.

"I'd rather die than—" Vivian said.

"Your death," the crow said, "is not yours to choose, clawgirl."

The crow, its third eye started to glow a crimson red. A glow that made Vivian tremble. Whimper terrified.

"No," Vivian said, "Not again ..."

And there was nothing Romeo could do—yet.

CHAPTER 2
ROMEO

No! There had to be something Romeo could do. Anything.

His whole body chilled at the thought of losing Vivian again. Having to fight her again. Maybe even hurt her again. All to somehow save her. Again.

But Romeo was paralyzed. Somehow. Like a mouse caught in a serpent's gaze.

Except the gaze—from that sinister crow.

No. Pa taught him how to escape that kind of gaze. Long ago. Back when a giant python was stalking the village he used to live in. It was a giant monster of a snake that ate several sheep a night and almost ate Romeo too.

Except pain. Intense pain.

At the right moment.

So right now, don't focus on the grunts and growls of the

gigantic beasts below them. Or how sweaty hot it was. Or even his own racing heartbeat.

Forget how Vivian and her fine, fine ass was so tense yet still pressed so wonderfully soft against his crotch.

Pleasure was certain death right now.

Worse than death for Vivian.

At the end of this long twisted branch that Vivian and Romeo both sat together on, the big fat crow in the moonlight, the crimson glow of that crow's third eye, he'd only have him a few more moments, he was sure of that, and using those moments right—critical.

So focus on the raw rough bark against his back. Poking his back through his vest. Through his slacks. His thick reliable suede boots. Not on the lichen and moss softening the mild discomfort.

No.

Focus on how, underneath that wonderfully rosy scent of Vivian, there was the sharp jab of the forest's musty smell, and that jab stabbing right up his nose each and every breath.

Like Uncle Jethron always said, trust your nose, and rely on it.

Don't focus on the other craggy branches around them. They hid them from most of the larger creatures around. That they were alone in this tree except for the crow.

At least, for now.

The other clawgirls from yesterday were sleeping in their own tree around the clearing. Best not put everyone in the same spot. Just in case of attack.

But they had thought, since, of course, they were clawgirls, that they could let out a warning call if one of them was attacked. Their reptilian underscent should have deterred the worst creatures from attacking outright, but ...

Yesterday it didn't deter the horse-sized jaybirds known as jumping raptors from attacking one of them.

And now, this crow ...

The pain of losing Vivian, of any of the clawgirls he just freed yesterday ... like a stab to the heart.

And enough for him to bite his lip.

HARD.

But he refused to whimper. Even move.

And reveal he freed himself from the crow's paralyzing gaze.

Until he pinched Vivian's thightastic thigh.

Hard.

WANT MORE?

Go to

WANT MORE?

Go to

www.JonathanEvanHudson.com

9 781955 880596